MW00940352

Happy reading
Marie Osburn Reid

THE SPIRIT BASKET

270 Years of an Alaska Family

by

Marie Osburn Reid

This edition is a revision completed in 2013. The original novel was first published as *Spirit Basket* by Author House on 2/9/2009.
Illustrations are by staff at Author House, Bloomington, Indiana.

(ISBN-13: 978-1481885774)

SPECIAL THANK YOU

For editing and encouragement a very special thanks goes to my husband Reford (Jeep) Reid, and dear friend Shirley Lewis Gordon. History was inspired by Dr. Molly Lee, and Dr. Aldona Jonaitis who is the Director Emerita at University of Alaska Museum of the North in Fairbanks, Alaska.

CONTENTS

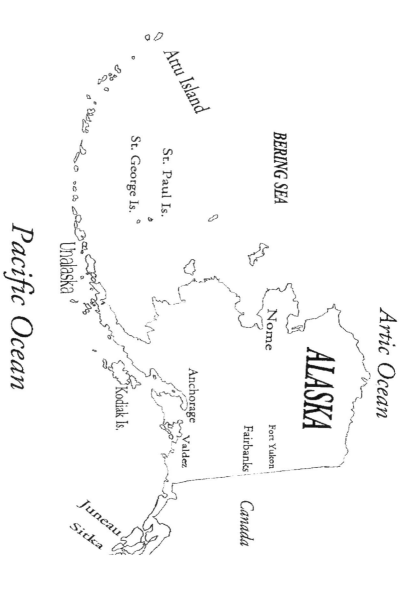

Attu Island

BERING SEA

St. Paul Is.

St. George Is.

Unalaska

Pacific Ocean

Nome

ALASKA

Fort Yukon

Fairbanks

Canada

Anchorage

Valdez

Kodiak Is.

Juneau

Sicka

Artic Ocean

FAMILY TREE

Attu Island – 1745: Angayuk (Aleut) son of the village chief

Aleutian Island – 1770: Tumgax (Aleut) son of Angayuk and Machxisa

Kodiak – 1794: Irina (Aleut), daughter of Tumgax and Morava

Sitka – 1834: Mikhail Zanskar (Aleut, Bengal) son of Irina and Richard

Sitka – 1867: Annarovia Zanskar (Tlingit, Bengal, Aleut) daughter of Mikhail and Neva

Nome – 1900: Peter Johansen (Swedish, Bengal, Tlingit, Aleut) son of Annarovia and Gustave

Fairbanks – 1925: Ivan Johansen (Athabascan, Swedish, Bengal, Tlingit, Aleut) son of Peter and Tana

St. Paul – 1942: Natasha Johansen (Russian, Athabascan, Swedish, Bengal, Tlingit, Aleut) daughter of Ivan and Lukenia

Anchorage – 1964: Luke Karlovich (Serbian, Russian, Athabascan, Swedish, Bengal, Tlingit, Aleut) son of Natasha and Anton

Valdez – 1989: Deborah Karlovich (Yupik, Serbian, Russian, Athabascan, Swedish, Bengal, Tlingit, Aleut) daughter of Luke and Ruth

Fairbanks – 2015: Jared Sheikov (Aleut, Yupik, Serbian, Russian, Athabascan, Swedish, Bengal, Tlingit) son of Deborah and George

PROLOGUE

Fairbanks, Alaska
The Year of 2015

My great grandmother made me come to Fairbanks to do this. June 2, 2015 is the most red-faced day of my life. Over 500 miles from home, I am carrying a big old basket uphill to a building that looks like the huge tail of a whale flapping from the University of Alaska. As tourists file into the museum, they point and aim cameras at me like they just spotted a bear cub.

"Wonderful basket! It looks so authentic," exclaims a snowy-haired lady wearing pink hat, pink shoes and, in between, pink everything.

"My ancestor's Spirit Basket," I say. The whole group surrounds me like they think this fifteen-year-old might spring into a Native dance right there on the concrete walk.

"Is it for sale?" drawls a man peering from under a Texas cowboy hat. He pulls twenty-dollar bills from his blue jeans pocket.

I'm rescued by a smiling lady who rushes like a kittiwake through the crowd. "You must be Dee Dee's little brother Jared," she chirps.

"Cousin." I correct her, but she flutters on.

"I'm Dr. Lee, the Ethnology Curator. Bring your basket and come with me."

I tag after her through tall glass doors at the museum entrance. She ushers me into her office. The walls are plastered with art. Some pieces are Native, a few are relics from the gold rush, but most are timeless and impossible to describe.

"My dad had to catch a flight to go back home, so he dropped me off here," I explain. It seems important that she doesn't think I was into lugging baskets all over the world. "I guess he called you, right?"

"Yes….yes….yes," she says like she's answering three separate questions. The first yes is with a smile to me. On second yes she takes the basket out of my arms. The third yes is with squinting eyes fastened on the raised pattern that circle the basket to simulate orca teeth.

When she pulls off the lid, a sensation creeps up my back and tugs at the roots of my hair. It's like something is released in the air. It smells of the sea, musty beach grass and a faint scent of berries. And there's something more spilling out. It's like a mist of tales passing through my nose to my head and into my heart.

"Tell me about your basket," she says.

"It's about two hundred fifty years old. My Grandmother Natasha says it was woven by her great, great, great, great grandma. I think that's about four greats, or maybe five. She says the basket began in the Aleutian Islands as an open basket and was later remade in Kodiak to give it a longer life. It has been as far south as Attu, east to Sitka, west to Kodiak, north to Nome, even to Fairbanks and Valdez. She tells us stories about our grandparents whose lives and spirits are woven in this basket. Grandma Natasha wants it to rest in a safe place like this museum."

Dr. Lee's green eyes were alight with excitement. "Can you tell me all the stories?"

At first, I can't answer. It seems like a tall order

because the basket was moved from one family to another through all those years. I think how the Spirit Basket was always there to witness the struggle to survive against hostile people, places and in disasters.

Those thoughts explode memories in my head like firecrackers. In some odd way I'm not here alone with Dr. Lee. Instead, I feel surrounded by spirits that bring all the stories into focus.

"I'll tell you the stories in the same way Grandma Natasha told me." They go something like this………."

CHAPTER 1

THE YEAR OF 1745
Attu Island
Russian America Begins
HARVEST OF THE FUR SEALS

"Look Ruuwaq (arrow), the seals have come!" Angayuk (buddy) called from the top of a knoll.

Angayuk could see the broad shoulders of his big brother pop up from hip high, coarse grass. Ruuwaq's moon-shaped face flashed with anticipation. He dropped a bundle of grass gathered for basket making and ran up the hill.

"Right you are, Little Brother!" Ruuwaq shouted into the wind. His wide grin bobbled the ivory labret fastened in his lip. "At last the seals have come."

"Let's get down there," Angayuk called, giddy with pride for being the first in the village to spot the return of the seals. Soon everyone would know. Their bare feet deftly picked the way between rocks down toward the pounding sea.

Fur seals lunged ashore. Sleek fur bodies spread over the rocks. Raucous barks and grunts rose above the thunder of waves that hammered the shore. With threatening snarls, huge males sparred with any that ventured too close to its band of females.

"When our summer days are longest, their numbers will grow to more than raindrops in a storm." Ruuwaq grinned with his chin held high.

"Then it will be time for harvest." Anticipation made a shiver run through Angayuk.

"Oh yes. Now that you have grown twelve winters, you will work with us as a man. Is your heart strong enough for it?"

With eagerness growing, Angayuk turned his gaze back to lively seals with countless birds circling over them. But then he spotted something in the distance. It was a sight that deafened his senses to barking seals and flapping bird wings. He nudged Ruuwaq and pointed at the strange thing sparkling far out in the water.

His brother's strong hand came down on his shoulder. "I see it too," Ruuwaq said in an unsure voice. "We must hurry. Grandmother waits."

Their tough-skinned bare feet raced over a grassy knoll.

Grandmother rested against a boulder that sheltered her from wind. Her busy hands twisted strands of bay grass for weaving a basket. Dark lines tattooed on her chin stretched wide apart with her smile. Squinting eyes trained on the boys glowed with delight. "Do I hear the barking of seals?"

"The seals have come and many babies are being born." Angayuk dropped beside his grandmother to receive her embrace. "Grandmother, something strange floats high on the water, coming close. It is bigger than a bidarka (canoe) and it comes to us."

Ruuwaq fell to his knees. "Grandmother, could it be that strange men from a far away land have come to our island?"

A look of urgency came into her gentle eyes. "You boys must be quick to run to the village. Go, run fast. Warn our people."

The boys sprang to their feet and ran through brush, rye grass, over pebbles and descended to the side of the island most protected from north winds. Here their people had dug into the earth and made dwellings of driftwood and sod. They ran by men who stretched sealskins over a carved driftwood frame to make a seaworthy bidarka. Women looked up from sewing shirts made of seabird skins using gut thread and bone needles.

Swift feet found their father, the chief, in the center of men huddled while he told a tale. His arms waved about as he told of the sights to be seen by paddling great distances, north and south, along the coast. His head bobbed so much that, on his carved wood visor, sea-lion whiskers wiggled like moth wings.

Angayuk burst into the circle of men startling them all to silence. He shouted, "A bidarka comes that is bigger than a whale!"

"It's true," Ruuwaq said, standing respectfully outside the circle of men. "We saw it from the cliff rocks."

All the men began talking in excitement. The chief ordered two men to lookout points. He told the rest of the men to fetch spears and gather up sealskins and seabirds for a possible trade.

When the lookouts returned, they reported that a huge boat with white wings like a giant bird bobbed offshore. Soon, every villager headed for the southern beach. The women carried baskets that held a few birds and carved bone ornaments.

While Ruuwaq walked with the men, Angayuk trailed behind with women and other children. He carried a strong basket made by his grandmother. It was filled with bird eggs.

Because the people were near the beach, everyone kept hidden behind low bushes. All eyes watched the magical bird wings billow out on tall poles above the big boat. Then, bit by bit, the whiteness crumbled down. The boat stopped sailing to shore. Strange looking men crawled into a small boat and paddled it toward the beach.

The village men erupted out of hiding onto the pebbled beach. In plain sight they held spears high and danced about. They yelled out in song, jumped into the air and twisted about to show the strangers they were both strong and friendly.

The paddling stopped. One of the strangers pointed a long, shiny black stick at the dancers. Strange words were shouted, but the dancers kept waving spears and danced all the more.

Paddling of the odd boat resumed and the shiny black stick still pointed at the dancers. When the boat crunched on sand, creatures with hair hanging from their chins, jumped out. All wore hats and their bodies, even their feet, were covered up with something other than furs or feathers.

The dancers stopped and showed jolly smiles. The chief gave a welcome shout and tossed a seabird and sealskin into the odd boat. It was a boat that was covered over in a wood like the kind that drifts on the sea.

At first the strangers looked surprised, but when one held up the sealskin, there was much talking. The one with the dark, shiny stick pointed at the chief and made motions with his hands. After many gestures to the sealskin, the chief nodded and flapped his arms to say there were many fur seals.

The stranger turned to the big ship and waved his black shiny stick. Another small boat came, paddled by strangers. They brought good things to trade.

Angayuk's grandmother insisted the basket of bird eggs to be traded for fine thread the color of a sunset. For the basket, he traded a thimble for his grandmother's thumb. It was hard like a clam shell and mysteriously etched with tiny, blood-red flowers. Other people were delighted to get a blanket made of something warm, a pipe and other things that seemed to have no purpose.

The chief offered a bone, carved like a sea otter, for the black shiny stick, but the hairy chin man shook his head and would not trade. All was peaceful until Ruuwaq tried to trade his spear for one of the small boats. The strangers yelled at him and pushed him away. One raised a paddle like he was going to hit Ruuwaq, but he was stopped by the sound of a big boom.

The boom was louder than thunder. All the people scattered. Angayuk hid behind boulders and others ran up the hill. Gulls squawked. Kittiwakes, puffins and other birds screeched. Overhead wings flapped in hysteria.

It was odd that none of the strangers hid from the horrendous noise. They just stood there. Angayuk stared at a faint stream of smoke coming from the black shiny stick. He was certain that had caused the loud boom.

The stranger with the black shiny stick shouted at the others. They quickly pushed their boats back into the water and paddled away to the huge boat.

Silence fell on the lips of all the people as they followed the chief back to the village. "These strangers have powerful weapons," the chief declared. "But their chief wants many seal skins. If we give them what they want, surely they will go away. A harvest will be tonight."

Everyone disbursed to prepare for the seal harvest. Angayuk felt a choking in his heart. "Is it too soon for the harvest?" he asked his uncle.

"There are some of those males who lose battles with the strongest bulls and won't get the cows. They are the only ones we choose to harvest."

Ruuwaq came beside him and said, "They're the ones we see at least two summers as they stay on the sands far from the others. Those are the ones that have no mates. Many are there now."

Grandmother nodded then looked into Angayuk's uncertain eyes. "You are old enough to help with the harvest this summer, my child."

"We must have the seal oil for lamps and for cooking," his mother said.

"Because you grow so fast, Angayuk, I'll need much seal gut for your new raincoat," Grandmother said.

Angayuk thought of the beautiful, sleek animals and how they feed and clothe his family. ""Since the seals are needed by our village, what will we do if the strange men come and take them away?"

"I'm sure they will take only some of the seals," his uncle said with little certainty.

Angayuk thought about the good gifts of the seals and he hoped there would be enough for the strangers and for the village. A dread gripped his heart.

When the time came for the harvest, Angayuk walked with all the others in the predawn dark. Thick clouds covered the moon. As he felt his way along the trail to the beach, in darkness, it was like an unknown place. The wind cooled his faced, lifted his hair back from his eyes and filled his nostrils with the smells of sea animals. The sound of the ocean splashed a steady slosh, slosh, slosh against the island shore. In the dark sky no gulls screeched, no wings flapped overhead.

He had never come here in the dead of night. Not until now. Angayuk gazed up at clouds beginning to turn pink in a sky turning toward dawn.

His father, the chief, bent near Angayuk's ear. "Darkness and the wind that blows our scent away will let the drummers slip in next to bachelor seals. While we wait here on the grass, our drummers hide along the beach until light comes."

The waiting people all around Angayuk tensed in silence as the dawn's first light touched the meadow. Then the morning exploded.

Yells, whistles, and drums pierced the wind as men descended upon the bachelor seals. Startled animals barked. Drummers slapped their moon shaped drums. Their voices sang out loud in fighting shouts. Angayuk was sure he could hear his brother holler. As seals scrambled, their fins propelled them away from the water and up onto the rocky shore. The hunters corralled them and skillfully let fly killing blows with clubs of driftwood.

Upwind the many thousands of seals gathered on the rocks appeared calm. The fracas at the far end of the beach passed barely noticed by that big herd. Angayuk was relieved that huge seal families nestled together would know nothing of the harvest. He was told if men were less skilled, the entire herd might panic and many babies in the big herd could be trampled.

The hunters were met with praise as they delivered the seals to villagers waiting on the bluff. Ruuwaq trotted up the beach with his arms weighed down by a limp carcass. He dumped it at Angayuk's feet and said, "The seals have given themselves to the people."

The people skinned and packed away the meat of each animal quickly. Everyone worked in an efficient team to prepare the meat and skins. Angayuk worked beside his family separating meat and fat from skins with sharp tools of stone. This work did not feel new to him because it was like cleaning fish, clams or crab. Those were things he did every day.

Raw, strong scented steam rose in the cool air. The pelts were bundled and tied with ropes made of seal gut so the men could pull the loads home. Hordes of birds settled in to clean the harvest field.

In the new morning light, a swirl of fog swept across tall grass and tiny bright wildflowers along the bluff. Angayuk got in step with a parade of bare feet headed back on a well worn path.

Angayuk's grandfather rested a hand on his shoulder. Pride and reverence glowed on his old, weathered face. "My grandson, this is as it has always been for the Aleut people and as it will always be."

This day would see a big celebration with dance and song to thank the seal spirit for bountiful gifts. But unlike any other day, men with hairy chins and ocean blue eyes would be there.

A fear swept from Angayuk's toes and settled in his stomach. He strongly suspected that life for the Aleut people may never again be as it was before.

CHAPTER 2

THE YEAR OF 1770
In The Aleutian Islands

ESCAPE

"Wake up, Tumgax. The rest time is over," Machxisa whispered.

Tumgax resisted his mother's gentle hand on his shoulder, but gave in when he heard the voices of Russian guards outside the sod hut's hide-covered opening. No matter how reluctant his arms and legs were to move, he must not put his mother in jeopardy. The guards might hit her if they sensed any disobedience.

He and his mother scrambled out of the sod hut. Machxisa offered him a strip of dried fish from her special Attu Island basket. Their rest had seemed only a short nap, yet they had slept too long. As his bare feet pounded over the cold muddy path, Tumgax chewed the hard fish. The last taste of it was gone when he reached his place at the skinning tables. His mother followed him in and stood beside him with a sharp Russian-made skinning knife in her hand.

Brisk sea wind whiffed in through cracks in the walls of the plank building. Tumgax was glad for the fresh air as it washed over the stench of wet blood, guts, and stacks of carcasses. His fingers and a blade separated flesh and bones from hide, moving without thought to the task for his mind dwelt upon a secret. It was a secret so daring that the bare whisper of it, if heard by a guard, would render him as lifeless as the seals and otters he scraped.

The *secret* beat in his chest, it ran through his veins. It was as much a part of him as the ivory labret inserted below his lip.

Years earlier Angayuk had said, "Be brave, my son." Tumgax was seven years old the first time his father was forced away on a Russian ship. In the five years that followed, father and son would be united only a few days each year when the *Nicholas* happened into port.

Tumgax thought of the story told by his mother with tears, and the one his father told with anger. Fur traders from a faraway land had come to their island. They brutalized and enslaved his gentle Aleut people. The fur traders slaughtered many thousands of sea otters and seals for markets far away.

The *secret* given to Tumgax by the shaman held

all his hope. With help from the great spirits, the *secret* would rescue his father, his mother and himself and guide them to freedom.

When the workday finally ended, Tumgax ran through the settlement and down to the beach. The Russians paid little attention to him, a mere child, now that his work shift was over. In the low tide, wet, cold sand pushed against his toes in the hiding places of clams and crabs. He gathered as many clams as he could hold. He carried them and a snapping crab away from the surf onto a path that twisted up a knoll.

Tumgax stopped at the shaman's sod hut where the mask of a red-eyed otter stared from above the entrance. The moment he placed the squirming crab and clams on the dirt floor, the ailing man struggled to his feet. He put a bony hand on the top of the boy's head.

"You are named for the walrus, Tumgax. So it is that a stubborn and mighty soul lives within you." The shaman's voice rasped. "Go far across the sea, away from these killers who bring death to our waters."

The shaman gripped a staff carved from a thin, crooked branch, and he flailed it in wide circles through the air. Tumgax kept his gaze on magical eagle feathers dangling from the stick; it banged against the earthen wall.

"Boy." Tumgax bent close to hear a whisper. The secret words puffed against his cheek. "In the eyes of your mind, do you see the hiding bidarka? Do you know the moonrock and sea wood that points the way?"

"Shaman, I have been there. I pushed away the bushes and driftwood to see for myself that it waits."

"Good, but go there no more until the time is right. The eyes of the evil ones are everywhere." Coughing came and took strength from the old man's tired body.

Tumgax helped him to lie on a bed of dried grass. The old man's weight pressed hard on his young arms. He placed a seal skin over the shaman and spoke close to his ear.

"I have heard sailors say the *Nicholas* is coming soon. This is the ship Father sails on. The time to escape comes near."

Weary eyes brightened in the flame that burned in a saucer of seal oil. "Remember to have patience, boy. But do not hesitate when danger strikes."

With those conflicting thoughts, Tumgax set about arranging the seafood in hot coals smoldering in a pit outside the hut. Then he left the sleeping shaman and ran through the autumn wind. He slowed to a walk as he neared the beach where wooden Russian skiffs lined the sand. A newly arrived ship was anchored off shore.

He brazenly approached a big bellied man with sea color eyes and a large red nose. "Is that the *Nicholas*?"

"That be the *Seamaid*. She waits for a load of pelts for the Orient. I don't expect a boy like you ever heard of places like Irkutsk or Canton. That right, boy?" The man grinned at him with yellow, decayed teeth.

Tumgax knew most of the Russian words so he politely gave a nod.

"That blasted supply ship is long overdue," the seaman complained. "So, it sure better get here with a barrel of good rum real, real soon."

Running away to gather more clams for his mother, Tumgax cried into the howling wind, "One day real soon!"

It took almost another month before excitement spread through the settlement. A ship from the north had landed.

Machxisa left her post at the skinning table, and Tumgax chased after her. This offense would normally be cause for harsh punishment, but the Russians rushed to the seashore too. They grumbled with hope the new arrival had vodka and barrels of rum to spare. Soon, all the workers, guards, traders, shouted and waved to men in skiffs who paddled toward shore.

In the last boat, one oarsman was not a Russian. There was no smile above the ivory labret on his lip. His back was straight, his stroke strong as he pulled oars against choppy water.

"It is he," Machxisa sang to her son. "It is Angayuk."

Tumgax had never felt more excitement. He wanted the three of them to run away from the crowd to the hiding kayak now, but he remembered the shaman's warning. He swallowed the *secret* back to silence.

The skiff's bottom scraped onto the sand. Men jumped into knee deep, cold water and pulled the boat ashore.

While men greeted one another with laughter and handshakes, Angayuk walked to where Machxisa stood. Their hands met and their eyes beheld one another. When, at last, Tumgax was noticed, a smile lit up his father's sun-darkened face.

"My son, you have grown and grown strong." Angayuk proudly grasped the boy's shoulders.

With so much to say after more than a year apart, they wanted only to walk and talk together. But the Russians had other ideas. There were barges to be loaded with pelts and three more hours of daylight left to work. The guards shouted and the Aleuts and the sailors went to work.

Tumgax and his mother returned with the others

to the hated skinning tables, but their hearts were filled with joy. Tumgax was bursting with the *secret*. He would share it tonight, at last.

When the sun had finally plunged into the sea and the clouds wore only a trace of color like burning embers, the three were free to hold each other. There were many months of things to say, but, for a while, all they could do was look and touch. Machxisa presented her husband with a *kamleika*, a gut parka, that in a drenching rain, the tight stitches would swell and keep him dry.

Angayuk held it up to examine it in the dim light from a flame of seal oil burning in a dish. He lovingly traced a finger over sea lion hair and auklet feathers that decorated it. "This is my good fortune."

Machxisa wiped at tears and moved heated rocks from the fire to water in the cooking basket.

From a hide covered bundle, Angayuk brought out a steel knife with a bone handle. "I've brought something for my son."

Tumgax's fingers caressed the marvelous blade. His throat barely let him speak, so in a bare whisper he said, "For a long time I have saved a secret to give to you, Father."

Angayuk's arm was around his son. He squeezed the boy to him. "Then quickly, tell me this secret."

"It comes from the shaman." Tumgax spoke in

excited words as all the details of the hidden kayak burst from him. As he spoke, his father stared at him in great surprise.

His mother gasped. "No, escape is too dangerous. At least here we are alive. Our son is alive."

Tumgax moaned. "To spend all my life working for the traders is not a life I want."

"The boy is right." Angayuk clenched teeth. "We owe him a try for another life."

"The shaman promises the spirits are with us," Tumgax said.

"Tonight liquor will pour from barrels. There will never be a better time than tonight." Angayuk put a loving arm around Machxisa. "Now is when we must go."

With a mixture of terror and excitement in her eyes, Machxisa removed fish from hot water in the cooking basket. "Now we will eat," she declared, but did not sit for the meal. Instead, she grabbed cooking and sewing supplies and stuffed them into a large woven grass basket. It was a special basket from Attu and woven by Angayuk's grandmother.

Tumgax barely tasted the cooked clams. His thoughts were in a fever. Would he be leading his family to a free life or to the end of life? This day their fate would be decided. He drew in a breath and vowed to himself to live up to his name. He would be as stubborn and mighty as a walrus.

As he pulled on his new *kamleika*, his father listened carefully to every detail Tumgax could tell him about the kayak and the path that would lead them there. Tumgax and his mother also slipped on parkas of seal gut that would protect them from the rains. Their only defense from the guards was the dark, cloudy night, and the Russians' craving for barrels of rum brought from Siberia on the *Nicholas*.

Tumgax walked boldly into the dark. A guard passing by merely grunted at him like he was a foolish boy. When the guard was out of sight, Tumgax waved a signal to his father and mother.

It was a calm night veiled in a low fog. Tumgax wished the howling wind would come to shield them as they had to pass within inches of the sailors' quarters. They fell to their knees to creep under windows.

When a door opened, muffled voices suddenly burst into bellows and three men staggered out. With arms draped about each other, the comrades sang a raucous song and tromped to the next building.

Another time, Tumgax might have laughed at their antics, but now he flattened himself and pressed his face into the tall, moist grass that smelled of raw earth. Angayuk and Machxisa did the same. They dared not move until a sturdy door slammed and the men were inside again.

They took to their feet. Although they moved as swiftly as foxes, the short distance through the settlement seemed endless to Tumgax. Finally their bare toes touched the cold pebbles of the outside beach. They scampered up to the grassy ledge to avoid leaving a trail on the sand.

In spite of the added danger, Tumgax led his parents to the shaman's hut. The red-eyed otter mask guarded the entrance.

"What is this place? Why are you stopping, son?" his father asked in an urgent whisper.

A weak, trembling voice rang out, "Boy of the Walrus, what do you bring me?".

Tumgax rushed in and whispered close to the old man's ear. "I bring my parents, Shaman. This is the night of our escape."

Angayuk and Machxisa stepped inside and greeted the shaman with bowed heads.

"Come, you must carry the feather of a seabird to keep you safe." He pulled open the ties on a tattered grass basket and removed three feathers. His gnarled fingers stroked each feather three times then handed one to each of them.

In return, Machxisa took a strip of dried fish from her basket and placed it before the shaman.

Angayuk said, "We go with gratitude for the spirit of good fortune."

"Then be gone!" He thumped the earthen wall with the feathered stick and waved them out into the night.

"The shaman's moonrock lies on the far side of the island," Tumgax said. "The shortest way is over the hill above the rookery."

"That is above the cover of fog." Angayuk frowned at dark clouds covering the moon, yet he agreed to follow his son.

Tumgax worried he might get them lost as he felt his way and strained to see the trail. Finally, he recognized a weathered snag with branches pointing like the shaman's old fingers. He knew they pointed in the direction of the enchanted moonrock. With certainty he said, "This is the way."

Machxisa stopped at the top of the hill, resting her basket on the ground. Tumgax paused beside her to look back before starting the descent to the south side of the island. Campfires cast a devilish light over the settlement that had imprisoned them for five years.

"Whatever is ahead will not be as bad as that," Tumgax said. His mother gave his hand a squeeze.

Angayuk did not join them in looking back. "Hurry, we must go."

The beach was rocky and slippery from foggy night air. Once again Tumgax began to feel doubt. All the rocks looked the same, how would he recognize the shaman's moonrock?

Just when his fears were about to spill from his lips, the boiling clouds parted and a ray of moonlight illuminated the shore. One rock stood out from all the rest in a soft glow.

"There it is! The moonrock that protects the hiding place," Tumgax cried.

He scrambled behind the translucent rock and pulled back bushes. There lay a skin boat with ribs of sturdy driftwood. It had space for three people and two paddles.

Hurriedly, they prepared to launch the craft. Machxisa sat in the middle where she could pass their meager supply of water, dried fish and seaweed from the basket tucked between her legs.

Tumgax took the bow. Angayuk pushed them off and settled in the back.

They were afloat. With the first strokes of the paddles the bidarka glided into the choppy sea. A wondrous smile spread across Tumgax's face. He turned to see his mother smile and his father too.

The moon spread a silver light over high rock walls. For an instant Tumgax thought he could see something embedded in the cliff ahead.

"Is that a spirit?" he asked with an arm outstretched. "I see a shadow that wears an otter headdress and waves that hit the cliff look like long fingers splashing out to us."

"It sends us on a safe journey," his father said. His mother sighed and gripped their special basket.

The family paddled north into the wind and waves of a new, free life.

CHAPTER 3

THE YEAR OF 1794
Kodiak Island – Russian America

THE GOVERNOR'S DAUGHTER

Irina hurried down the path through the rain forest known for many huge brown bears. In a light breeze from the sea, the scent of spruce trees filled the damp air. Lush fern leaves brushed against Irina's faded skirt. Her mother, Morava, had sewn the skirt for this special day, making it out of old flowered material. The cloth had been bright red and yellow when it came to Kodiak village from China. That is when her mother's needles had turned it into a dress for the governor's wife.

There was a great need for fabric to be reused again and again in this time of shortages. Supply ships had not come for nearly four years. But her father, Tumgax, who had seen many seaports, said that things would soon change because of the Russian Tsar, Catherine the Great.

The thought of what those changes may be, gave Irina goose bumps. It was exciting. It was scary. The scariest thing was that her best friend, Anna, was madly in love with Captain Rezanov. Today was Anna's fifteenth birthday. She was less than two year older than Irina.

The snap of a branch startled her. Thinking of the monster bears that lived on the island, Irina twisted about in fear. A stranger, a boy of about her age, stepped out of the thick brush.

"Good day, Miss," he said with a mysterious accent and a slight smile.

Irina's fright turned to annoyance. "May I ask just who are you?"

"I am Richard Zanskar." He spoke with each word in measured Russian.

Irina looked him over. He was not barefoot like an Aleut. He wore boots that fastened with straps and were soft, not the hard leather of Russian boots. Instead of a Russian hat or a seaman's knitted cap, fabric wrapped his head just above his ears. His pants ballooned above his boots and his silk shirt shimmered in the summer sun. His bronze skin did not look Russian or Aleut or Tlingit.

"I have not seen you before," Irina said. "My uncle, Alexander Baranov, spoke of a British ship that brought flour. He said a new mast is being built for it. Did you come on the *Phoenix* from Calcutta, India?"

The boy blinked. "You speak words I do not know as yet."

Irina could tell he barely understood her Russian words, so she repeated all she had said in Aleut. He looked more confused than ever and replied in a language that was unintelligible to her. She shook her head and giggled. He shook his head, too, and his broad smile gleamed with straight, white teeth.

Irina said slowly, "Where do you come from, Richard?"

Richard jumped up on a fallen tree and pointed toward the dock. "The ship."

She used pointing fingers to touch her heart then gesture to land. "I am from here, Kodiak. What land are you from?"

"Land far away." Richard stretched his arms to the sea. "It is Bengal."

"Then will you sail back to Bengal or India soon?" Irina guessed he must have been a cabin boy on board the ship.

Richard hopped off the log. "Captain Moore says I stay to serve Sir Baranov..... to speak the English for him."

"I'm impressed that you speak both English and Russian."

Richard's black eyes twinkled. "I talk words of Bengalese, German and England and…" He pinched a finger and thumb together with little space in between. "A little bit Russia."

Irina realized how distracted she was and brushed passed him on the path toward the governor's grand house. "Perhaps we will meet again."

"So what name is yours?" he called after her.

"I am Irina."

She promptly forgot about the interesting stranger, and her fretful thoughts turned to Anna. A week ago, Anna had begged her to come for tea this day to meet Nikolai Rezanov. Anna had said he was a nobleman from Russia sent by the Tsar to help Governor Shelikhov prepare the colony for coming priests and laborers. With a swoon, she described him as tall, lean, handsome and so very cultured. He knew languages, namely French, and played the violin. Anna had inherited her father's tendency to exaggerate, so Irina scarcely believed there could be such a man.

The hardened mud path turned into a boardwalk leading to the governor's grand house. Like a mansion, it sat loftily atop a knoll cleared of trees and overlooked the town, harbor and sea. A bronze knocker with the face of a lion adorned the oversized door. When Irina's fingers gave it a bang, she pressed an ear to the boards and heard running footsteps. Instead of a butler, Anna pulled the door open.

"You're here at last, Irina." Anna clasped her smooth, pampered white hands over Irina's brown, hard-working fingers. "I need to talk with you."

With Anna's blond curls bouncing before her, Irina followed her up two flights of well polished stairs. Together they danced into the bedroom of white lace and pink ruffles.

"So, what do you need to talk about?"

"Well, I need to know how I look." Anna held out her skirt like bird wings ready for flight and she twirled around. "Does this dress make me look older? A more mature lady?"

"That shade of blue is good with your lovely blue eyes." Irina felt a pinch of envy over the dress. "But why do you want to look older, Anna?"

"My fantastic gentleman friend, Nikolai, is thirty years old." Before her large oval mirror, Anna stretched as tall and straight as she could. "I can't wait for you to meet him today."

"He's twice your age. Oh Anna, are you really hoping to marry him?"

"Well, Irina, exactly who else on this island would my father give his consent to marry me?"

Irina shook her head. "I'm amazed that there is anyone in the whole world he would approve for his dear daughter. I can't see why it would be Captain Rezanov."

"He greatly admires Nikolai for being a true nobleman, acceptable in royal society. Besides, Father is terribly impressed that Nikolai promises to plea with the Tsarina for permission to let Father set up a Russian American Company."

"I don't understand a word about all that, Anna."

"Nor do I." Anna giggled. "They talk about it, going on and on endlessly about trade with China and such things."

"My father talks mostly of hunts for fur seals and fur otters with Manager Baranov." Irina sighed with a show of boredom. Her thoughts briefly leapt to her father, Tumgax. He greatly helped make fur hunts for the Russian colony successful because he could translate the language of the Aleuts. As a boy he had learned to speak Russian when he was held as a slave by fur traders. That skill endeared him to both Mr. Baranov and Aleut Chief Kenaitze.

"Frankly, I must marry him," Anna declared.

"Oh?" Irina's attention focused completely on her dear friend who stood before a mirror as she pinned long, soft curls atop her head.

"Years and years could go by before another Russian ship might bring a more desirable man to the island."

"You haven't known him for more than a month. So how can you guess what your life with him will be like?"

Anna flopped onto her bed and Irina crawled on beside her. They lay staring up at the lacy canopy.

"With him, we will sail away to our fatherland, to Saint Petersburg," Anna said dreamily. "In the city I will attend grand balls, the theatre, attend church in a cathedral, ride in carriages and meet important society people."

"You will leave Kodiak. You will go away from me forever." Irina swallowed back a sob and sat up.

"Not forever. I'm sure Nikolai will want to visit Kodiak often."

"I hear it takes a whole year to travel to Saint Petersburg," Irina moaned. "By then you will forget me."

Anna threw her arms around Irina. "You helped me learn so many things. Would I play the piano without you? Or crochet? Or write poems? Or make baskets and bead necklaces? You are my true friend."

Irina smiled at the exaggerations. They had practiced many skills together, but Anna was adept at few.

"I made you a present." Irina reached into her pocket and presented Anna with a tiny basket. Its lid was embroidered with red and green silk thread. "I made this for your birthday."

"It's so sweet. You and your mother are the best basket makers in the world." Anna hugged the basket to her heart and gave Irina a vigorous embrace.

Such praise seemed beyond appropriate to Irina, but she loved her friend all the more for it. "May it always remind you of our friendship, no matter how far away you may go." She kissed both of Anna's cheeks.

When the birthday tea began, Irina was introduced to Nikolai Rezanov. She found him cordial, but felt the attributes by Anna were overstated. He was too tall. Anna's head barely reached his chest. His face was much too long to be handsome. When Anna's mother requested he play a violin concerto, Irina found it squeaky, lacking in melody and it dragged on far too long.

After that day, Irina brooded about losing her friend and school mate. For sympathy she turned to her mother. Morava twisted and intertwined long strands of grass as she said, "I was a girl of fifteen when my father, the chief of our Aleut people, gave me to the great hunter Tumgax. Look at the fine things that union brought to our lives, these walls, cook stove, sink, cushioned chairs, and good beds."

"But Mother, Anna lives so well in the finest house. Why does she want to go away?"

"Ah, but she is Russian. She longs to have the luxuries her mother knew in Siberia," Morava said.

Irina shook her head. She did not want to hear her mother repeat the town gossip about the lavish house Governor Shelikhov had built so his family could live with great pomp. To change the subject, Irina quickly picked up fresh strands of grass that smelled of summer.

"Mother, this will be a wonderful big basket. How clever of you to preserve great grandmother's basket in this way," Irina said. She picked up the tattered basket that was woven in the ancient way. For more than fifty years, it had held fish, birds, berries, many things. Now it held only pieces of bones and ashes of ancestors.

Morava grinned. "Tumgax holds onto the memories in his great grandmother's basket. His dearest hope is to honor her final wish that someday the sacred bones within will be returned to Attu Island."

"You are adding a beautiful lid with red silk threads that look like the teeth of a killer whale."

"Signs of the Orca will keep it tough. With a strong, new body the Spirit Basket will last forever." Morava continued to twist strands of grass.

Before the end of the summer, Irina was not to hear the announcement of her dear friend's betrothal first from Anna herself. The news came when she was in the home of her Uncle Alexander Baranov.

It was a dinner party with her uncle at the head of the table and Auntie Baranov at the foot. The table was overburdened with roasted meats and fish. Smokey aromas permeated the curtained room of handmade furniture. Places at the table were filled by a British sea captain with whom her uncle spoke in German. An American first mate sat next to him. Irina was beside Mr. Kuskov, a man with a wooden leg and talents for ship building. Across from her was her father, mother and Richard, the boy from Bengal that she had met on the path. The conversation was loud among the men who talked of ship riggings, tar and building supplies.

Irina had no interest in such talk but her ears strained to hear when Auntie leaned close to Morava's ear. They murmured sisterly things to each other but Irina heard Auntie's excited words. "My dear sister, you will soon have to sew a beautiful white dress. The Shelikhov girl will wed in January, the day after Orthodox Christmas."

Irina's appetite vanished. Her knees went as soft as pudding and her drumming heart drowned out the men's loud voices.

Her gaze went across the table to Richard's dark, long lashed stare. "It has been many weeks since me met, Richard, but I see you are still here in my Uncle's home."

"I will go away soon, but not for a long time." His turban was a bright orange and his shirt silky white. Irina was surprised he learned to speak Russian well in such a short time.

"If you sail away to your homeland, the journey will take many months."

"No. We go in the sloop *Olga* to search for a new place to build a colony."

Her Uncle Baranov chimed in, "Ah yes, the *Olga* will test my skill to navigate. Kuskov, Richard and I will sail south." He raised a cup of rum. "Here's to exploring as far as the sound of Sitka."

The men responded by all talking at once. They offered warnings of stormy autumn seas and tribes of warlike Tlingit Natives.

Irina was glad when she could gracefully leave the table. She did not need to help clean up as there was kitchen help for that. Escaping outdoors, she settled on a porch bench and watched the full moon reflecting off the bay.

"A silver moon tonight," a voice behind her said. Richard was silhouetted in light from the open door. "Why do you look with sad eyes."

"Anna is my good friend. She will be gone away after the wedding. I will miss her greatly."

Irina saw concern reflecting in dark caring eyes. "It would make me glad if you let me be your friend."

"I see you are treated like a son in my uncle's house and have been given a room here. That must mean we are cousins." Irina gave him a teasing smile.

He sat down beside her on the bench. "So, you will lose a friend, but you have gained a cousin."

Irina laughed and feelings of true joy returned.

CHAPTER 4

THE YEAR OF 1834
New Archangel, Sitka

THE PRIEST

In the Aleut language, the Russian Orthodox priest commanded, "Master Mikhail Zanskar, please remain in your seat after class."

The sound of his name boomed through Mikhail from his ears to his toes. He froze in his seat.

Forty-one boys, ages eight to fifteen, dutifully laid down their slates that were scribbled with math figures. All hands became folded and eyes were fixed on the bearded instructor. With a nod from him, all except Mikhail stood up and formed a single file line then obediently walked from the room.

Mikhail fidgeted. His bony bottom had kept the hard bench warm for endless hours. His dark stare remained glued on amazingly tall Father Ioann Veniaminov. Blue-green eyes stared back from a head known to be filled with the biggest brain in Unalaska or in all of Russian America.

Pondering how and why the priest was about to find fault with him, Mikhail thought hard about yesterday and days before. Those days had been in this classroom where he passed exams with high scores. Yesterday, when the setting sun cast long shadows on the sea cliffs, he gathered bird eggs with his friend Timofei, who was the son of the priest. In the evenings, Mikhail's sharp knife whittled until the snout of a sea lion appeared on a hunk of whale bone. He could think of nothing he had done to provoke the stern, but fair-minded, priest.

Fr. Veniaminov began to pace the room with his eyes dancing from walls to ceiling. "Mikhail, you are my best student. You have learned the Gospel well in both Russian language and Aleut." Mikhail thought about how this priest had brilliantly written down the Gospel so the people in his village could learn to read it in Aleut. "And you also know Bengalese, the language of your father. Am I correct?"

"Yes sir. My father is from the continent of India."

"Ah, it is because words come easily to you that I believe you can be quick to learn another language." The priest brought his gaze down from the rafters to the boy. "I want you to learn Tlingit. With that knowledge you will be a help to me in the Sitka Islands."

"Then…. it's true that you are moving away to New Archangel?" Mikhail clasped the bench with both hands to steady the room that seemed to shake with anticipation.

"I'm sure everyone in Unalaska has heard that Governor Wrangell wants me and my family to join him there to improve schools and work with the Indian population. The Tlingit nation is remarkable. You will be as highly impressed as I when you see what they do with trees."

"Me?" Mikhail gasped at the thought of himself aboard a ship that would sail hundreds of miles from home.

"You are fourteen years now, a year older than Timofei. Both of you will be a great help to me." With his big hands folded behind him, Fr. Veniaminov bent his long body toward the boy and grinned. "Do you agree?"

"I'd like to see trees growing on a land," Mikhail blurted, with a thought of driftwood and that no trees were on his island. "I would like to see other places."

"Very well, speak to your folks. Tell them our study of the Tlingit language begins tomorrow after class. We must learn before June." With that Mikhail was dismissed.

Stepping outdoors, raindrops hit Mikhail's brown face that felt hot with excitement. He turned away from the schoolhouse the priest had built.

A strong wind blew off the sea. It flattened tall grass and thrust against Mikhail's seal-gut parka. His bare toes slid over moist pebbles on a worn path and dug into hard mud. He passed many partly buried sod homes that made dents into low hills.

Mikhail's home was a mix of driftwood and sod. He found his mother, Irina, sewing by their only glass window. She wore a blue, straight-line dress of cloth brought to the village by Russian ships. Her long hair was tied back with traditional Aleut beads.

The instant he entered, Mikhail poured out his whole conversation with the priest and ended with, "I want to go with Fr. Veniaminov. Then he can teach me about making a sundial watch and a flute. He knows everything."

His mother frowned. She touched his arm with a squeeze as if she wanted to hold onto his short, wiry body. He was the youngest of her seven children. "Governor Wrangell is not concerned with the priest making such things as clocks."

"There's no end to what the Father can invent." Mikhail handed her a skein of thread that had tumbled to the floor.

"The governor wants him to teach another priest in that village how to make Christians of the Indian people." Irina picked up a needle and squinted as she threaded it.

"I heard what you are saying, my son." Mikhail's father, Richard, appeared from the next room where he often read books. He pulled a faded, rust-colored turban off his graying hair and hung it on a peg by the door. "It would be a good thing if the clever priest also teaches you to make furniture, Mikhail."

Irina sighed and set aside her mending. "The Tlingit people can be dangerous. They fight to keep the ways of strangers away. Even the courageous Father Veniaminov may never make them his friends."

Richard put a calloused hand on Mikhail's shoulder. "Many years ago, Governor Baranov and I found that to be true."

Mikhail smiled. "Tell me again the story of how you went by sea from Kodiak to Sitka Island."

A broad smile full of even, white teeth lit up Richard's face. He took a seat next to Irina and held up two fingers. "We had two ships and hundreds of kayaks when we entered Sitka Sound. Sir Baranov traded beads, brass and bottles to the Tlingits and we built a fine settlement."

Irina sighed. "Yes, but remember what happened there after you and my uncle returned to us in Kodiak. They destroyed the colony and nearly every settler was killed or made a slave."

Richard nodded, but his black eyes beneath thick brows glistened. "Baranov did not give up. We sailed back and rebuilt the settlement behind a strong stockade."

"Much has changed," Mikhail argued. "Everyone says Governor Baranov made the town of New Archangel safe long before he died."

"Irina, your Uncle Baranov was a good man," Richard said.

Mikhail held his breath as his mother threaded bead after bead into a colorful woven design. Her eyes were cast down when she finally uttered, "Tell me no more about it until you learn the Tlingit language. That is the only way you can be a help to Fr. Veniaminov."

Mikhail's grin beamed with straight, white teeth like his father's. He stretched his arms to the sky. "Thank you!"

The next morning Fr. Veniaminov, in his gregarious way, was delighted that Mikhail would be a volunteer. "I welcome your help and it will be good for Timofei to have his best friend with us."

Over the next months the boys and the priest spent nearly every evening in the company of two Tlingit Indians who had been seal hunters for the Russian America Company. The priest was a demanding teacher but was usually gentle at the same time. As they studied together, he told Mikhail and Timofei, "The Tlingit people are difficult, but are clever and smart traders. They are to be admired."

Timofei squirmed in his seat. "How can we admire them if they worship birds and animal gods?"

Mikhail was not surprised to hear that from his friend who was sandy haired and a head taller than him. Timofei always wanted to hear the stories about the adventures of Governor Baranov and Mikhail's father in the Sitka Islands long ago. He was horrified to know the Tlingits attacked the colony.

The priest gave his son an intent look. "These people have much to learn about Christ, but their art and culture is greatly advanced compared to many other Indians in the world."

"Mikhail said the Tlingits killed hundreds of colonists and made some of them slaves. I wish we were going back to Siberia instead." Timofei's mouth curved in a pout. "That's what mother wants too."

"What happened there was a long time ago," Mikhail said.

The Father placed a compassionate hand on his son's back. "In New Archangel your mother need not labor to teach reading. She will enjoy more leisure there."

Mikhail beamed with deeply felt admiration. "Everyone on our island reads now that you have given us a dictionary for the Aleut language."

The priest gave a hearty laugh. "And now lets learn a new language together. Get out your slates."

When the ship came to port, Mikhail hurriedly gathered his few belongings. Irina insisted he carry the ancestral basket filled with all she could stuff into it. At high tide the ship was ready to leave. Mikhail's father and brothers were somewhere out at sea paddling kayaks in search of fur seals. Only to his mother and two teary-eyed sisters were there to wave him off. The sight of them disappearing in the distance left a pain in his heart. He knew it would be a very long time before he could see his family again. Perhaps that would never be.

Mostly the voyage was on moderate seas. Gentle waves slapped against the ship's wooden hull, and sails flapped in the stillness of early morning. On the sixth day, the ship bobbed toward the mainland known as Alaska.

Unusual terrain came in sight. Mikhail and Timofei shared astonishment at the forest on the edge of the sea.

"Can you smell that? Trees, real trees," Mikhail shouted and filled his chest with long breaths. The scent of spruce and pine was like the walls in his village church that were built of the lumber that Fr. Veniaminov had shipped from a faraway place.

"Those trees are bigger than I saw in pictures of Siberia," Timofei exclaimed. "We need to climb to the treetops!"

"Look!" Mikhail exclaimed as bright sunlight sparkled off astonishing sights. "See what the Tlingits have done with trees."

The shoreline erupted with a row of houses, all made of wood. Beached in front of the houses were carved, fiercely decorated wooden boats.

Timofei jumped up and down and pointed. "Over there is the town that has a fence all around it."

The boys and everyone on board the ship cheered happily at the welcome sight. Enclosed behind a stockade embedded with cannons was a spread of buildings, a church with a steeple, and on a hill was a very large home.

"That is Baranov Castle. It's the governor's mansion," Fr. Veniaminov announced. "And I do believe that is Governor Wrangell who comes now."

From the harbor, three boats paddled toward the ship. When the boats were alongside the ship, a short man with a bright red beard stood up and called, "I am Baron Ferdinand von Wrangell, Governor of Russian America.

Everyone on the ship responded with excited waves and called greetings.

"You must not come to shore until everyone on board is vaccinated for smallpox," the governor briskly shouted. "Those cursed American whalers have spread much sickness through the population."

"We were all vaccinated in Unalaska," Fr. Veniaminov assured him. With ease, he pulled the governor aboard.

Governor Wrangell wore boots with heels that he snapped together with a click when he stood at attention on the deck. His shoulders were wide and back stretched as if straining for as much height as possible. His tall hat barely reached to Fr. Veniaminov's chest as he shook hands with the priest and gave a formal nod to Mrs. Veniaminov.

In a steady voice of authority the Governor announced, "Welcome to New Archangel." Then he turned to everyone on board. "Do not go beyond the walls that encircle the town. That stockade is there to keep hostile Indians out."

After a short conference with Fr. Veniaminov, he invited the family into small boats to be rowed to shore. Mikhail climbed into a boat that was very different than the sealskin and driftwood kayaks he knew. It was made of honed planks of wood. As they reached the shore, it bumped against the dock with the bottom scraping on pebbles in shallow water.

Buildings adorned with many windows loomed large on the shoreline. Pathways were filled with men pulling carts or riding bicycles, children playing, and women walking in long dresses. Mikhail itched to explore the town. But he dutifully followed the procession along a boardwalk that took them to a wood house. The governor told them he had it prepared for them.

Mikhail carried his big basket into the small room assigned to him. He lovingly ran a hand over the bright red teeth design on his ancestral basket. It was a comfort to have this one thing to remember his family. With his eyes closed and the voices of his mother and father swimming in his mind, he promised himself to keep the basket near him always.

Until the family was settled, the governor insisted they all dine at the mansion for evening meals. This gave the priest and the governor time for planning, and it gave them all the treat of roasted venison and music. Mrs. Wrangell and a daughter played a grand piano and a violin. The sounds were so loud and foreign to Mikhail he wanted to cover his ears. Unlike Mrs. Veniaminov, whose pale face spread with smiles and eyes closed with pleasure, he wanted only to escape. Rather than sit politely on a cushioned chair, he longed to run across the polished floor and outdoors into quiet, open air.

By the third day, Mikhail asked to be left behind rather than go to the mansion again. He promised to keep busy with getting the church ready. The church was an old ship that Sir Baranov had converted when the Russian government sent the settlement its first priest. With its well-carved ornaments and vestments of colorful beadwork, the altar was more elaborate than the church in Unalaska. Yet Mikhail knew Fr. Veniaminov had already started to draw plans for a big, new church.

Mikhail climbed to the roof with a rag and bucket of water to scrub green moss off the bell. He was just high enough to peer easily on the other side of the stockade. The dark clouds and rain of the day had passed. A cool wind swept off the water.

In the summer light of evening, Mikhail looked down into the Tlingit Indian village. A fire on the gravel beach roasted meat and filled the air with a scent like the kitchen in Baranov Castle. Women turned a hind quarter of a deer on hot coals. Men squatted together in conversation. It was a peaceful scene until a woman screamed and ran out of a house carrying a naked child. A man waving the mask of a shaman chased after the screams. He hollered words that Mikhail interpreted to mean, "Child burns with evil."

The woman wailed all the more and plunged the child into the tide. Its black hair spread out on the water. The mask with a bird beak wagged back and forth as the shaman grabbed the lifeless child. Mikhail could not make out his words. The woman stood on wet sand, weeping. Others ran to the her, coaxing her away from the tragic scene.

The church bell gave a startling, "Bong!"

Mikhail jumped and realized he had leaned into it while spying on the Indians. When he straightened up, it banged again, loud enough for the whole town to hear. He ducked down hoping no one on the beach could see him. He could see Tlingit men look his way, and one angry fist was raised in the air.

On legs that felt unsteady, Mikhail climbed down from the belfry on a rope ladder. When he was out of the church, he heard voices. The family had come home.

"Did you ring the church bell?" Timofei said, running to him.

Mikhail kept silent until everyone except Timofei and Fr. Veniaminov had gone into the house. Then the story of what he had seen tumbled out.

"I think the child died," Mikhail struggled to say with a lump in his throat.

"No doubt it was smallpox," Fr. Veniaminov said bowing his head prayerfully. "I think it is time for us to visit that village. Tomorrow morning I'll tell the governor that we will go."

"Tomorrow?" Timofei asked with his eyes wide with fear.

The compassionate father touched his son's shoulder. "I'm sure your mother will need your help tomorrow. Mikhail will go with me."

"Yes sir," Mikhail said, trying to sound braver than he felt.

The next day, Mikhail waited outside the mansion in a light rain. When Fr. Veniaminov appeared, looking all the more like a giant in his full vestments, white robe flowing from his broad shoulders and lofty headdress that covered most of his unruly hair. He was followed by Dr. Popov in a black coat and derby and holding a doctor's valise. Four soldiers trailed behind carrying rifles.

The Father's big boots pounded on the boardwalk. His thick brows knitted together over a distressed glare.

As if ordered by the priest, the rain stopped. A rainbow arched over the town and Mikhail felt like a crusader as he proudly followed along. The parade passed a university, trade school, warehouse and ship-building yard. When the wooden walk ended, the soldiers hurried ahead to unbar the gate in the stockade wall. Father Veniaminov raised a hand to the soldiers. "You men wait here for our return."

The soldiers nodded and stood at attention facing the Indian village.

"But the governor said…" Dr. Popov protested.

"We will walk with God, not soldiers."

"I don't know. That can't be wise." The doctor stepped back against the fence.

Fr. Veniaminov stroked his beard thoughtfully. "Then give the serum to Mikhail. He will carry it to the dying children." He turned on his heal and stalked down the hill.

With the chilling memory of the child's hair floating in sea foam, Mikhail grabbed the valise from the doctor and ran in the tracks of the priest's broad stride.

Dozens of small wooden houses lined the beach. The priest walked directly to the largest building painted with a grotesque bear. Its red tongue hung down to paws with claws made of copper. Mikhail lingered close to the priest's robe and the bear's ugly face.

People gathered around. Women huddled together with babies strapped to their backs. Children clung to their mothers' leather skirts and fringed shawls.

Most men wore hats made of woven spruce root or wood carved with the head of a bird or animal. Some walked toward them from decorated boats on the beach. Others strode from homes with copper ornaments. A few men carried spears. Their faces were bold and shone with scorn.

Mikhail glanced back at the three cannons in the stockade that targeted the village. The soldiers were still there, but that didn't help him breathe easily. He tried to concentrate on the words the people spoke to each other, but he could not interpret. All he could think about were the looks of anger, fear, and deep sadness.

"I come as your friend," Fr. Veniaminov announced in their language with a gentle voice, and his arms stretched out to them.

The sun broke through dark clouds. Rays of bright light glistened off his white robes. The tall bearded man towered over all. "I am your friend." He paused and looked from one face to the next. "I come here to protect you and your children from the smallpox disease."

"What is this? What trick?" called out the shaman. He pointed the bird-beaked mask at the priest.

"It is called vaccination," the priest answered kindly. "With it, a child who is not sick will not get the smallpox."

A woman wrapped in a blanket and wearing beaded fur moccasins rushed forward with her arms around two children. "Shaman danced and called to the gods. Yet, two of my sons died, my husband died and my sister too. Only these two children are left to me." Her pleading voice cracked.

"Then bring them to me. Bring them here," the Father ordered.

"I must try," the woman said. She pulled her children forward.

"I will bring my son too," said another. But the two women were the only ones who came forward. Others fell back and gathered around the shaman. The men with spears circled the priest and Mikhail. They watched carefully but did not interfere as Fr. Veniaminov chose a long, sturdy log for his clinic.

The two anxious mothers scowled at the men with spears. With determination they led their children forward. The women received shots first.

"Be brave," Mikhail mumbled as he held out each child's arm for Fr. Veniaminov to puncture with needles. "Just a little bite like a mosquito will keep you well."

Every few days, Mikhail and the priest returned to the village. They found the vaccinated children and their mothers still healthy. Others fell sick. Gradually more people came to Fr. Veniaminov for vaccinations.

By the end of summer, the epidemic appeared over. A few Tlingits began coming to church services. Mikhail knew they came because the priest made them as welcome as anyone.

Governor Wrangell asked what the secret was to win the hearts of these strong-willed people. Mikhail knew he would forever remember the secret. The gentle words of Fr. Ioann Veniaminov rang in his head. "In order to influence the heart, one must speak from the heart. Then the hearts of listeners will find your words hard to resist."

CHAPTER 5

THE YEAR OF 1867
Sitka

THE COMING OF AMERICA

After October 18, 1867, New Archangel would be known simply as Sitka. On that rainless day, dust rose from the streets in glittering yellow specks before the setting sun.

Annarovia gazed at her tall, handsome mother as they walked together along the pebbled beach. Beyond a line of many brightly colored Tlingit boats, they could see Baranov Castle in the heart of town.

"It is right to dress well for this day," Neva said. She brushed her fingers through the fringe on her sleeves.

"Your skill, Mother, has made this dress of deerskin my favorite." Annarovia sniffed the raw scent of the soft deer hide.

"Do I see your face filled with too much pride for the beautiful beads you have sewn on it?" her mother teased.

Annarovia's pale skin flushed. "Mine doesn't have the fine fringe nor as many beads as yours." She brushed her hand over rows of intricately beaded flowers on her mother's back.

"Today is special." Neva took her daughter's hand.

Their heads turned toward the top of the hill where the good governor, Prince Dimitrii Petrovich Maksutov, his wife, and five children gathered with military men near the towering flagpole. The lovely Princess Mariia did not show her usual joyful smile.

"The beautiful princess holds her baby and I'm sure she looks sad," Annarovia said. Her thoughts went to all the talk in town filled with worry. "Will the Russian Company move away when the land goes to the American general?"

Her mother answered with an uncertain sigh. They walked to the edge of the murmuring crowd and stood silently to show respect.

Drums began to beat. Russian sailors and a battalion of soldiers came marching through the town, up to the knoll and across the parade grounds. They stood at attention before the prince and the Russian imperial flag that hung limply overhead in the blue sky. Another set of drummers approached, followed by two American generals trailed by over 200 marching soldiers. On command, the Americans stopped in a lineup before the flagpole. A trio of Russian soldiers stood at attention at the flagpole and held onto the rope they would use to descend the flag.

A sudden boom fractured the air. It came from a cannon fired from the *Ossipee,* an American ship anchored in the harbor. Russian cannons answered. The flag inched downward.

The cannons were followed by rifle fire. American soldiers fired round after deafening round into the air. The pungent scent of spent gunpowder washed over the crowd.

Abruptly the cannons and artillery stopped. A stunned silence fell over all.

"What is it, Mother?" Annarovia squeezed her mother's hand.

"Look how they struggle with the Russian Imperial flag." Neva gestured at the flagpole where soldiers tried to unsnarl rope.

The flag had stopped coming down. It appeared hopelessly tangled. A Russian soldier flipped the pulley rope, fighting to free the flag. When this failed, other soldiers boosted him up the flagpole and he caught hold of the emblem. He slashed a knife into twisted rope. The flag fluttered down impaling itself upon bayonets raised in salute by the Russian battalion.

Neva clung to her daughter. "This is surely an

omen."

"Oh," Annarovia gasped. "Look how Princess Maksutova has fainted."

The princess lay crumpled in the heap of her black satin gown. All ceremony stopped as Prince Maksutov and a doctor bent over her. Gradually she revived, and with help weakly returned to her royal chair.

"What kind of omen does it mean, Mother?"

Rumblings swept among somber fishermen, merchants and soldiers. "Perhaps, trouble will come." Neva's eyes widened with worry.

Once the rope was repaired, an American general gave a command and activity resumed. The raising of the United States of America flag was smooth. Stars and stripes rose quickly up the flagpole. The Russian general declared the Territory was officially turned over to America.

American soldiers gave three cheers. Cheers did not come from the crowd. All remained respectfully quiet until the prince's carriage was loaded with the royal family. As horses pulled them away, all uniformed officers and troops marched off the town square.

When people began to disburse, Annarovia heard a man nearby say, "Now we stand upon American soil."

Annarovia turned to her mother. "Why does no

one seem happy about the change?"

"Some Russians object since the Tsar wanted to sell Alaska to pay for a war his country fights. Americans may object because the cost for Alaska was an enormous sum, more than seven million dollars."

Annarovia felt very puzzled. They walked through town toward their home in the village. The whole town seemed to smell of fresh-cut lumber. In the heart of town, men had resumed working with hammers and saws. New, spruce log buildings lined the rutted dirt road. "I don't see why so many Russians say they will be leaving now."

"Everyone is uncertain, worried about what changes will come," her mother replied. "Only newcomers from America may welcome this change."

That evening, Annarovia persisted with questions to her father, Mikhail, who said, "Nearly seventy years ago, the Indian people gave up fighting the Russian traders because many lives were lost to cannons, rifles, and to sickness. My father was here when Chief Sha-yut-lelt traded land with Lord Baranov and the town was built."

"But that was only here on Sitka Island. What of the rest of Alaska?"

Mikhail could only tell her about a small corner of Alaska. His stories were of his life in Unalaska, some ports along the Aleutian Chain, and in Sitka with the famous priest, Father Veniaminov.

One day in the weeks that followed, Annarovia discussed this with her teacher, Mrs. Petrokov. It was the end of the school day and the other students had gone. Annarovia always lingered to tidy the classroom and, afterward, she helped to clean the chapel and do other chores for Mrs. Petrokov.

She asked in the Russian language, "How could they buy this land when it belongs, not to them, but to my people?"

Mrs. Petrokov, who was the wife of the Russian Orthodox Priest, laughed and patted the girl's glossy black hair. "My dear girl, I'm sorry to say Indians cannot own land. Not under the Americans."

"But why?" Annarovia fought an urge to slam her dust cloth to the floor.

"Because Indians are not considered civilized." Mrs. Petrokov impatiently flipped the pages of a worn book of English translations of Russian words.

"I'm Indian and glad to be."

"Annarovia, I find you very bright, and, being Indian or not, you deserve to learn reading and writing."

"Will learning to read and write English allow me to have land in my own country?"

Mrs. Petrokov sighed wearily. One hand brushed a spray of caulk dust off her long black skirt. Her other hand smoothed the bun in her brown hair. "Speaking the language of America may win you a man one day who owns land."

Annarovia wagged her confused head. "With all the Russians leaving Sitka, there will be no white men with land left here."

"There are American men, hundreds have moved in already. It will be important to know their language."

"Oh, no. I'll want to die before marrying an American." Annarovia fought to hold back all the mean words in her thoughts. She was expected to be polite, but still she said, "They bring smallpox and trade rum to my people."

The teacher nodded sadly. "I agree the Americans are a curse on this land. They've thrown out our good Russian laws and left us with no laws and no protection."

Annarovia thought of the many stories of Russian treachery her father told, but Mrs. Petrokov was not at fault. She did not deserve painful words. "I wonder what will become of us?"

Sighing again, Mrs. Petrokov gave a shrug. "Enough for today, my dear Anna. Please clear the classroom and then you are free to go home."

With her mind barely on the task, Annarovia gathered up books on the classroom tables. She stacked them neatly, as she did every afternoon when all the Russian and Tlingit students were gone. Then she wrapped a shawl over the shoulders of her wool school dress and stepped out into a light drizzle.

The village was on the outside beach, well beyond the edge of town. A thick pine forest formed a barrier between townspeople and villagers. When the village was in sight, Annarovia stopped to gaze at it with pride. She could see her father, Mikhail, chip away at a massive cedar log that he brought from an island far to the south. He was carving something like the Indians in southern villages make. Since Sitka Island did not have cedar trees, no one here had ever done it before. Mikhail called it a totem pole.

Splinters of wet wood covered over rain-soaked grass around her family home. The figure of a big-eyed bear topped the totem pole. When completed and erected, the bear, a dolphin, a salmon, and a frog would look out to ships passing in the bay. Annarovia asked her father why he worked so many months on such a difficult pole.

"Each figure tells a story about your mother's family. It is a good way to keep the stories of Indian people alive," her father explained. As a boy, Mikhail learned many skills in woodcarving from the clever priest who built the beautiful church in the heart of town. "I hope someday totems will be carved to stand in front of other homes in this village."

"But why would the Tlingit people ever accept such a change?"

A smile of remembering flashed on Mikhail face. "I will speak to them from my heart and they will learn the wisdom of a totem pole."

At that moment a breeze blowing up the beach carried voices through the village. Mikhail snapped attention toward the noise and grabbed hold of his hatchet.

A woman screamed. Men shouted out curses.

Annarovia knew of drunken white men in town who sometimes beat their Indian wives. But this was her village. Something was terribly wrong.

"Anna, run to the house. Now," Her father commanded.

She ran across the village clearing and burst through the doorway of her home. Inside she stopped in shock. Taku, her eight-year-old brother, crouched under their table with a long-bladed steel knife. It was her father's knife.

"Taku!" Annarovia scanned the darkened room until her mother's wet eyes shone back at her.

"Your brother is protecting us." Neva's lips moved with a fearful quiver. She gripped a sewing needle and continued taking rapid stitches in a garment spread across her lap. "Drunken soldiers wander in the village making threats."

Annarovia slumped on the floor before her mother and stretched trembling arms around her.

Shouts from outside began to fade and soon quiet came. Mikhail entered the house. "They're gone now. We persuaded them to leave. Hunta had a rifle." He walked to his son and took the knife from Taku's small hand. Mikhail gazed thoughtfully at its fine bone handle as if remembering the day long ago when his grandfather Tumgax gave it to him.

"I wish I had a rifle like Hunta," Taku snapped, his Aleut-Russian-Bengal-Tlingit face flushed.

"Rifles are for hunting animals, not men." Neva's motherly voice was steady and reassuring.

The darkness of a storm cloud washed over Mikhail's face. "There may be no man in the village who believes that any longer. Danger from the American soldiers grow. Hunta speaks of an Indian army."

"Good," Annarovia blurted. "It's time our people took possession of the land. The land is ours."

Both her parents stared at her. It was her father who spoke with quiet conviction. "People cannot own the land, the rivers, or the sea. These things may only be our friends or our enemies."

Her mother quickly turned away and resumed sewing tense, little stitches. Though she was silent, Annarovia suspected her mother understood her feelings about owning land.

In the weeks that followed, tension in town and in the village increased. But the strain was not simply between soldiers and Indians. It was also between the longtime Russian citizens and discontented soldiers sent from Washington without instructions on how to govern. Assaults happened, thefts and even murder passed without arrests.

Annarovia's bitter teacher told the class. "Beware, children. When laws do not exist, only the meanest or strongest will survive."

On a snowy Friday morning in late December, Annarovia found no Mrs. Petrokov or students in the classroom. Books were neatly placed on the shelves as she had left them the evening before. How could it be that no one had come to school? It was time for class to start.

A premonition sent a chill over her. She dashed from the classroom and over the snow-splashed path to the Chapel. The glass in a window was broken out. Pushing hard on the heavy front door, it opened upon an altar in ruin. Golden icons were stripped from the walls, carvings smashed, and a red velvet altar drape pulled to the floor.

Annarovia trembled. Her father, Mikhail, had helped build this church for Bishop Veniaminov. Her stomach felt sick.

Carefully, she picked her way through debris and on to the Petrokov family quarters. She tapped on the brass door-knocker. She expected to hear the click of shoes crossing hardwood floors and a cheerful call. That did not happen.

A man's voice from behind startled her. "Hey, Little Girl."

Annarovia spun about to see two American soldiers. One was taller than the other. Both were young, clean-shaven and not carrying rifles. The tall one spoke in a gentle tone.

"You're not going to find anyone at home in this house. They sailed out on the *Nena* last night."

Timidly, Annarovia carefully chose words in English. "The priest is gone? Where did they go?"

"I suspect to the Mother Land," said the tall one with sad eyes. "The American congress granted land to all who became citizens within three years, but they keep leaving. A couple hundred sailed out of here for Russia last night on the high tide."

"We're sorry to say they were scared away by bad rampaging soldiers," the shorter one said with a deep frown. "But this time they've gone too far by tearing up a church. This time the General will have to do something about it."

"It's gotten out of hand, that's for sure," the other said. They talked to each other as if Annarovia was not there numbly gazing up at them.

The shorter man nearly shouted with indignation. "Even some Americans who came to

Sitka to build are giving up and shipping out."

Then the tall one knelt down and spoke gently to the girl whose eyes were fixed on his mud caked boots. "You run along home now, Little Miss. There's nothing for you here."

Annarovia walked home with a heavy heart. It had started to rain on the snowy road. One horse drawn wagon passed her, its wheels slipped through slush. The quiet of the street, that had been so noisy weeks earlier, was eerie and sad. She hugged her weather-tight coat of duck feathers against the gray print dress Mrs. Petrokov had discarded and insisted she wear to school.

"They're all gone," Annarovia cried in Russian. "The teacher and all of the pupils are gone," she spat out in precise English.

She stomped her deerskin boots in a muddy slush-puddle. Anger and bitterness stayed with her even when she came to the edge of the forest. Her feet slipped over the snow-crusted pebbly beach. Seagulls squawked at her. The village looked clean and white. The brightly painted totem lay finished beside her home. But even the thought of the potlatch to raise the totem pole did not cheer her.

The minute she was in the house she cried, "Father Petrokov has taken his family away. They sailed on the high tide last night without even a good-bye."

Taku gave her a startled look as he unfolded a bright red blanket fringed in deer hide. "What makes them go?"

"I heard the good Father has been called back to the great cathedral in Saint Petersburg," their mother said.

"I'm sure the real reason is fear." Tears spilled down Annarovia's cheeks as she fell to her mother's knees. "Mrs. Petrokov is right. The town is no longer safe."

"It is safe here in the village." With a soft cloth Neva gently wiped her daughter's cheeks.

"Thanks to Hunta, the Americans are afraid to come here," Taku boasted.

"So you say, Little Brother."

"You'll find out tomorrow at the potlatch," Taku said, then he burst out of the house with the red ceremonial blanket about his shoulders.

"There is much to be done, Anna," her mother said. "The totem pole is to be celebrated. All clans, Eagles and Ravens, will come from upriver. There are geese, salmon and berries for us to prepare."

Neva handed her daughter a big basket that had been woven by the great-grandmother. Its tight weave was from the fine bay grass that grew in their ancestor's homeland far to the north at Kodiak. The air sweetened with the scent of dried raspberries as Annarovia lifted a full bentwood bowl from the basket. She sprinkled them with water and added spoonfuls of American sugar.   Gently she stirred the red fruit into sweet pulp. Her memory replayed the happy days when her family and friends went to sunny hillsides to pick berries.

Annarovia thought about the potlatch that would go on for many days. She and her mother had carefully made bentwood bowls for gifts. As each family accepted a bowl, it would be showing approval for the totem pole. The pole would be raised at the entrance of their home. Her father called it, "As in the Indian way."

Succulent aromas would fill the smoke from open fires that cooked shellfish, salmon and strips of venison. Voices would be raised in songs from the ages. Storytellers would wear beautiful button robes, each decorated with the emblem of a clan. The abalone buttons, beads, and yarn would form the stunning image of a black raven, eagle in flight, or hungry wolf.

Men, women and children would all dance. The finest beaded slippers would tap and stomp, tap and stomp, until moisture dripped from every brow. Some would wear elaborate headdresses and everyone their finest clothes. Carved hats would have the faces of a proud eagle, mischievous raven, or happy whale. Perhaps the down of swans would flutter from the dancer's hat like swirling snow. Annarovia had seen that once. She also longed to see an elder do the dance of the grizzly bear wearing a bearskin with its claws sheathed in glossy copper. Drums would beat. All the dancing feet would be strong, powerful, ancient, enduring.

"Mother, when all the clans come together, there will be many, many more warriors than all of the American soldiers. They will always protect our village."

The misery of the morning left Annarovia's heart. Her spirits lightened with pride for her people.

CHAPTER 6

THE YEAR OF 1900
From Sitka to Nome

GOLD NUGGETS

"Here in lovely Sitka, fish and game are plentiful. Why does my son seek more?" asked Peter's mother, Annarovia, as she gently touched his arm.

"But, I have passed fourteen winters. I am strong and old enough to explore in the world," Peter Johansen pleaded with his mother and also with his Uncle Taku.

The burning fire outside the big lodge cast a dancing light onto frog eyes on the totem pole. Uncle Taku gazed at the carved figures one at a time as if deep in thought. He turned to Peter and glared as woodenly as the chiseled bear. "These islands provide our people with all desires."

Under that glare, Peter shifted his gaze to the open sea. Gentle waves sloshed a restless melody against the rocky beach. He spread both arms toward the waves. "Captain Clancy tells of many wonders in the world that cannot be seen from here."

His uncle squinted at the misty, gray sky. At that moment, an eagle alighted atop the totem's head of the bear. The eagle flapped its magnificent wings then settled to a watchful perch.

"Your Swede father was like this Captain Clancy. He sailed away to look for nuggets of gold in the sand, never to return." Taku was as firm as the sure-footed eagle.

With a stick Annarovia moved clothing submerged in a pot of water heating on the fire. Peter could see his mother's injured spirit. It came from waiting these last six years for his father's return. For a while Peter had longed for his father to return too, but he set his mind to shake off that wound.

Worry was set in deep lines around Annarovia's lips. "Do you not hear the priest warn this is a trail pitted with evil?"

"Mother, I hear many things. I want to see the land of my great, great grandparents. If I go north with gold seekers, it will be my chance."

Little by little Annarovia's face brightened as a thought formed. "Perhaps you could carry the labret and bits of bone that hold the spirits of Angayuk and

Machxisa. My father's promise to his grandfather will be fulfilled if they can be returned to the island of their birth."

"Then that is as it will be," Taku declared in a tone that ended the discussion.

Peter sucked in his breath to contain his excitement. At this moment he knew he must show only respect. His uncle and his mother fixed their gaze on a hollowed-out cupboard in the totem pole. In a well carved bentwood box rested the spirits of Angayuk and Machxisa. Peter knew the unfulfilled promise was a debt that had long burdened the family.

Annarovia retrieved the box and bowed her head. "My son will bear the ancestors' spirits to Attu."

Peter put his arms around his mother and squeezed her to him. He felt her stretch up to him with pride.

A flap, flap of powerful wings broke the quiet. The flapping eagle launched from its perch atop the totem pole. It flew into a sunset that burned red and gold over the sea.

"See that? The eagle brings a good omen." Peter smiled happily.

A week later when the tide was at its highest, he bid farewell to his Uncle Taku and both of his young sisters and left them in the village. Annarovia accompanied her son to the dock in Sitka. Standing beside the steamer, *Columbia*, she handed Peter the big basket that had always been very valuable to the family. It had passed down from Annarovia's great grandmother on Kodiak Island. Now the basket was filled with supplies Peter would need and one thing more.

"Within this special basket is the box where the spirits of Angayuk and Machxisa sleep," Annarovia said.

"I will carry the ancestor spirits to Attu. I promise you that, Mother."

"This big basket is tight, secure, and a thing of beauty." Her finger traced over the intricate pattern of red, spiked Orca teeth.

Peter wrapped the basket into his bundle and swung it onto his back. He shifted his gaze to the deck of the ship where the captain and crew hustled about. "I know Mother, I'll keep it safe." He tried not to show impatience, but his mother could never be hurried nor fooled.

"Then go, and leave me with only my daughters." Tears welled up in her eyes.

Peter's heart overflowed with love for the woman who had persisted in teaching him words of English and Russian and the ways of their village people. He put his free arm around her. "You will always be in my heart, Mother."

Captain Clancy's gravel voice called his name.

Peter ran down the dock and jumped on board the *Columbia* as it slipped away from the dock.

Peter dropped his bundle on the deck and grabbed hold of a tie-down rope, one of four that needed to be coiled. As he worked, his excitement was overshadowed by the watchful little woman in a beaded deerskin dress. He knew a vision of the proud figure alone on the shore would tug at his heart all the days of his life, no matter where adventure might take him.

Captain Clancy came up behind him, pulled his cap off thick, wind-whipped hair. He wiped his sleeve over perspiration on his brow. With a good-natured swat of his cap on Peter's back, he asked, "Hey, Lad, did you tell your mom you'll be back in half a year? That, right after Nome we'll head back?"

"I did, Captain." Peter looked up at the lean man with sky-blue eyes streaked as if with a red sunset.

"Well, it's good your family let you sign on to my crew. You're a lot younger than any I had before, but you know the sea. I need that. Also, I need someone who won't jump ship in Skagway with all those fools running after gold."

"You can count on me, Sir," Peter assured him.

When the *Columbia* steamed up through the inside passage to Skagway, Captain Clancy had no choice but to relent and allow his men to go ashore. While the rest of the crew hurried off the ship, Peter remained to finish loading supplies delivered on the deck. He was more interested in the Captain's expectations than in sightseeing.

In the late afternoon, a piercing whistle blasted away. There came a steel-ripping screech echoing off the mountains surrounding the seaport town. The new railroad had recently been completed and served to take gold seekers over mountains, glaciers, and rivers into the interior of the Yukon. A puff of steam billowed like a tiny cloud above the town.

What was happening in Skagway was too exciting to resist. Having to see the train for himself, Peter jumped onto the dock and set out at a run.

Through a haze of spruce-scented smoke, Peter spotted Captain Clancy on a grassy knoll crowded with onlookers. The train slowly chugged into town exhaling smoke and smelling of pungent grease. Another blast of the train's whistle sent a charge through Peter's bones and a wide grin to his face.

"Captain," he cried. "Someday I'll be a rider on one of those."

"I don't doubt that you will." Captain Clancy chuckled at the rapture-filled eyes glued on the massive beast of iron.

"That train chugs right up that mountain so easy. It's so big, bigger than a pod of whales. What power! I could look at it all day."

"Well, all day won't work today, young man. The tide is coming in. Help me round up the crew."

Reluctantly, Peter turned away from the noisy, beautiful machine. He and the captain meandered among gold seekers and townspeople to coax deckhands to return to the ship.

At the dock cargo destined for Nome was delivered, so the crew got busy and loaded it aboard the *Columbia*. On the high tide they slipped anchor lines and sailed away. Fortunately, just one crewman was lost to the lure of gold fields.

It was a peaceful sail as they made way through the protected waters of the Inside Passage. Peter felt content with the deckhand routine. He caught fish, cleaned the galley, and felt cold salt spray on windy nights. He listened to sailor yarns about faraway places and watched them play poker with their wages. Quickly, experience was making him a good sailor with valuable know-how.

As the *Columbia* moved out of the Inside Passage into the open sea, small waves grew into large heaving swells. Slowly, tall mountains faded into shrinking gray shadows and seemed to disappear into the sea behind the ship. In all directions there was nothing to see but waves of water.

After eight days in the rolling seas, the *Columbia* neared the Aleutian Chain. A blast of wind abruptly twisted the ship off course. The bottom seemed to drop out of the ocean as the ship plummeted down a steep wave. Then, when the next wave hit, the deck shot up again as if it had wings. Peter fought for balance on the turbulent deck as he worked with two sailors wrestling ropes to secure cargo.

"Where'd this miserable storm come from?" shouted a sailor named Buck.

The other shouted, "I never saw it coming. It just hit. Bam, like that!"

Another gust of wind and another huge wave lifted the ship's bow toward angry clouds. Peter shouted above the wind, "My grandfather said that sudden storms in these islands can tear a ship to pieces."

"We could use a little Indian hocus pocus right now," Buck said. His weathered face tightened in near panic.

Peter tugged on ropes helping the men tie more knots around the cargo. The raging sea filled his mind with stories he heard in his childhood. The old tales cast doubt in his mind sending a strong worry over him. He wondered if he had offended a spirit in some way, perhaps the spirit of a sea creature. Fear sent Peter searching the black water, raging foam, and for dark cliffs. He looked for the unseen.

"There is a safe glacier fjord somewhere near," he shouted with confidence.

Smirks of disbelief crossed faces. Buck bellowed, "Kid, there's nothing out there but the black sea."

Peter wondered why he made such a rash prediction. Since this was the first time he had ever been in these waters, how could he know of any fjord? But a certainty came from somewhere deep within him.

With the ropes on the cargo tightened, Peter and the other two fought against wind and gripped the rail as they pushed on the pilothouse door. The ship took a plunge on the downside of a wave that stood higher than a giant spruce tree. A whirlpool of foam swept the three of them inside then a gust of wind slapped the door shut in time to keep out a flood. Wave after wave sloshed against the pilothouse, throwing Peter and all other sailors to the floor.

Captain Clancy managed to remain upright as he gripped the wheel, fighting to keep it from spinning out of control.

When Buck got his feet planted on the floor, he said with a smirk, "Hey Captain, the kid's been giving us a little of his grandpa's hocus pocus."

"Well, Peter, I wish your granddad was here right now. Maybe he could give us a clue," Captain Clancy wailed.

Peter pressed against the window. All he could see between attacking waves was a dark mountain peak on what must be an island. Something was odd about the peak. He wondered what it could be until the ship was lifted on another giant wave.

"There, off to the right!" Peter shouted. "Snow above that cliff is a glacier."

Through layers of tumbling clouds, a flash of sun beamed onto the river of ice nestled far into a hilly island. The seamen knew that many glaciers reach the sea after centuries of cutting a path. Water within the narrow passage of a fjord would be protected from high waves.

The crewmen sighed and shouted with relief as the ship twisted and tossed closer to safety. "Kid, you've got the eyes of an eagle," Buck shouted.

When the *Columbia* settled into choppy water laden with icebergs, Captain Clancy shook Peter's hand, "Good going, Lad."

Peter felt oblivious to the Captain and the others. His head throbbed with ghostly visions that plagued him from the moment he had spotted the beam of sunlight reflecting off the glacier. Something like a shaman wearing a red-eyed bird headdress had floated in frothy waves. The figure reached with watery fingers that splashed out from black rocks.

Wondering if it could be the ghost of an ancestor, Peter vowed to keep the vision a secret. Mysterious visions may happen when fear sees strange things in a storm. He was certain that for the rest of his days on earth, he would remember and wonder.

The storm lasted throughout the day and into the night then vanished as quickly as it had come. Several times Peter thought he would ask Captain Clancy if he could use the skiff to take the ancestor spirits to shore. But, each day after chores to restore and repair the battered vessel, he fell into exhausted sleep.

One morning, Peter felt the ship shift into forward motion. He grabbed the spirit basket from under his bunk and rushed onto the deck. The ship's bow was headed into the open sea. Captain Clancy shouted orders for full speed ahead.

Peter retreated with his basket of sacred cargo. Tightness gripped his chest. In the few words he knew of his great grandparents' language, he said, "Someday, I will take you to your home."

He pushed the Spirit Basket back under his bunk, took a deep breath then bounded up to the deck.

As the *Columbia* navigated through the Bering Sea, waves remained tumultuous but manageable. In ten days, the settlement of Nome was in sight.

The ship was anchored off shore as there was no dock at Nome. It was two days of off-loading cargo before the crew was granted shore leave.

In a drizzling rain, Peter and Captain Clancy

paddled the skiff into shore. Peter was astonished at the sight of the beach strung with equipment and tents. As Peter pulled on the oars, the Captain explained that gold-panning and sluice box operations were set up to find gold in sand lying on the beach.

"Be careful, Lad. Don't brush too close to any of that junk. I know you got light skin from your Swede dad, but those gold-crazy critters might shoot you without asking since you dress in hide pants like an Indian boy."

Peter felt the sting of that warning. On the docks in Sitka, he had experienced distrust of his race by foreign crews. And among his people, there was the same distrust of white men.

"Why do people not like someone who is different than they are?" he asked as they plodded by creaking wagons that inched through rutted streets.

His question was drowned out by a thunderous clap of sand and gravel into sluice boxes and street noises in the city of Nome. There were scrapes and screeches of shovels in beach sand. Wagon drivers shouted at their horses and each other. From a saloon, a piano plunked an odd tune. Raucous songs spilled out to the wooden walkway.

When Peter held his hands over his ears, Captain Clancy laughed. "Best get used to the racket. It'll go on around the clock since the summer sun doesn't set in Nome."

Peter's hands switched abruptly to cover his nose. "What stinks?"

"The sewer runs in the alley," the Captain said with disgust.

Peter was surprised to see the city of Nome was much bigger than either Sitka or Skagway and many times uglier with thousands of shacks and tents edged close together on the beach. Peter could see passengers and cargo off loaded from ships into rowboats because there was no loading dock here on the Bering Sea. He glanced back at the beach lined with men who worked with shovels and crudely made sluice boxes. Beyond the buildings and tents at the edge of the beach there was no forest. The treeless, rolling hills were covered in bush. Peter thought this place very different from his forested home so far away.

Clancy stepped into a place selling tobacco. Peter waited on the street filled with puddles and deep mud. A horse-drawn wagon was stuck in a mud hole. The driver was a man with a bushy mustache, an oversized belly poked out from his black poncho, and gold rings sparkled on his stubby fingers. He called to Peter, "Boy, come here. Put your shoulder to the wheel. I'll make it worth your while."

Peter didn't hesitate to give the man help. With a hard push on the wagon and steady pulling by the scrawny horse, the wheel bounced onto firmer ground.

"Good show, Kid." The driver took out a black satin pouch. "Catch this."

Peter snatched a pebble from the air. Opening his hand, he saw a gold nugget the size of a large garden pea.

"Thank you, Sir," Peter called after the clattering wagon. "Look Captain, this is gold, isn't it?"

Captain Clancy grinned as he rolled tobacco in thin paper to make a cigarette. "That should buy your supper, even at Nome prices."

They entered a cafe that was half tent and half board plank. The menu printed in chalk on a board next to their table offered a choice of fish or reindeer stew. Both of them ordered the stew. Sitting across from him, Peter decided the Captain's ruddy face had taken on a glow of excitement.

"I have half a mind to stay here for most of the summer, Peter," Captain Clancy said. "Of course, you could sign on with another rig going south. But I'd be mighty pleased if you wait until I'm ready to sail."

"I'm in no hurry. If I can find some work around here, I'll stay too."

"I'll see to it. I know where they'll welcome a

strong kid like you."

The waiter brought them wild blueberry cake, and the Captain paid the bill for both of them. Peter thanked him saying he was glad to not part with the gold nugget.

"Maybe you've just begun collecting nuggets." The Captain laughed.

In the weeks that followed, Peter followed Clancy's advice by packing his hide clothes away. He dressed in overalls to work at unloading vessels and sweeping out the Dexter Saloon. The saloon was an evening favorite with men who worked the beach sand for nuggets and flakes of gold. On his first day at the saloon, a dancehall girl gave him a tip that would provide Peter with a modest gold mine of his own.

"When a drunk opens his poke to pay for a drink, bits of gold dust often spill to the floor," the woman called Stella told him. She was like a goddess clothed in flowing sea foam. Her lips were bright red, her hair pale yellow. Sparkling stones dripped from her earlobes. "Peter, you'll do well to collect that dirt in a bag."

Peter took her advice seriously. He wrapped the sweepings up in a cloth every night. He carried it back to his bunk on board the ship. Every few days he had enough to pan and wash out grains of gold. Gold dust began to fill a pouch.

As time passed, two dreams would visit Peter when he lay down to sleep. One was of his mother, hands raised, reaching after him from the shore. The other was frightening enough to awaken him, perspiration running from his brow. Images from the storm at sea returned, ever reminding him of his unfinished task. He became convinced his ancestors were haunting him.

As summer ebbed, the night sky gradually turned from sunny blue to black speckled with stars. Captain Clancy avoided Peter's questions about shipping out before freeze up came until one day the Captain admitted he had invested in a gold claim on a creek a few miles from Nome.

"With the gold I get out of that creek, I can live like a king in Frisco. We'll head south again next summer. You can work the creek with me, Peter."

Peter was not prepared for such a change in plans, so he gave no reply. Instead he took a walk along the beach. The nice woman, Stella, told him of one ship that might hire him on if he wanted to sail for home.

The *Tobias* was anchored in the bay. Peter took the skiff that Captain Clancy allowed him to use for fishing and to travel daily between the shore and the *Columbia*. When he rowed along the side of the *Tobias*, he hollered at a crewman.

"Is the Captain there? Are you hiring on?"

A burly man, with a wool knit hat pulled down to his bushy eyebrows, appeared on deck. "I'm looking to hire men, but not kids. Where you wanting to go, kid?"

"Sitka, with a stop at Attu on the way."

"We're heading for Siberia and on to Hawaii then back to San Francisco. We got business in those places."

Peter didn't bother to boast about his sailor skills. He resolved to let the *Tobias* sail without him and pulled on the oars toward shore. Flock after flock of ducks, geese, and plovers squawked above him. They flapped their wings in the faded blue sky, making great loops in preparation for long flights south. With a deep sense of regret, Peter resolved to tough out the winter in Nome.

Winter was a grim time for Captain Clancy. He never got a chance to work his claim. When snow buried the creek, the Captain's dream fell to the corruption of lawless Nome. Claim jumpers moved in and ordered the Captain out, rifles pointed at his heart. The court proved futile since the judge was one of the claim jumpers.

One evening the saloon was crowded with men glad to be out of the fierce wind blowing off the frozen sea. Peter was wiping up tables when Captain Clancy's boasting caught his attention.

"I traded my tub for a paddle-wheeler docked at

St. Michael. Come May, I'm heading up the Yukon River. They say the streams that run into the Yukon River are lined with gold." Captain Clancy picked up the cards dealt to him. Men across the table argued the merits of such a plan.

When the days grew long in the month of May, and the sea ice gradually left the bay, Peter examined his pouch of gold dust and knew he had enough to book passage to Attu, the land of his ancestors. But his heart beat with excitement when the Captain spoke of the Yukon River. It was an adventure he could not miss. He knelt beside the basket that held a bentwood bowl of the sacred spirits.

"The day will come when you are returned to your land," he promised. As he touched each orca whale tooth circling the lid, the timeless design trembled through his fingers. Closing his eyes, he spoke in the words of his great grandparents, "Taga quliin! Someday, this I <u>shall</u> do it!"

CHAPTER 7

THE YEAR OF 1925
Fairbanks to Seward

RETURN

Ivan Johansen choked back a sob as he pushed up the old trunk lid. There was the sturdy basket with its tight lid safely concealing a bentwood box. In the box were ancestral bits of bone. Like ghosts they haunted his father Peter now, more than ever, in his dying moments.

"Are you taking great grandpa and grandma to Papa?" whispered Bessie, her breath white in frigid air. Her tear-swollen eyes swept with fright over the spirit basket.

Ivan nodded as he brushed passed her and out of the storage shed. On the snow-crusted path to their log house, six-year-old Timmy ran up to him and flung his arms tightly onto his waist.

"What will happen to us now?" Timmy was not wearing mittens.

"I will take care of you." Ivan pulled firmly away from his little brother and stepped into the warm, spruce scented one-room home.

Three men in mud-splattered clothes stood about the room. They had carried Peter Johansen from the mine and placed him on the couch. Boiling coffee sat on the hot pot-bellied stove. The men sipped coffee laced with whiskey. Glancing at Ivan, Bessie and Timmy they continued talking to each other as if children were no more than pups.

Okie Jim talked with words flowing slowly, like a lazy stream. "Ain't it a crying shame these little kids are losing their daddy after their mamma done passed on less than a year ago."

"Damn shame," agreed Red, the one with a beard the color of fire. "That cave just gave way, killing those other two good men instantly and leaving this one here crushed. I'm feared nothing's going to save him now."

Shorty, the one with a big stomach, said, "Lucky fact they're Indians. Them redskins know how to get along, even little tikes like these."

"Till Dad's better I'll take care of Bessie and Timmy," Ivan said loudly. The gold miners turned to him.

"Mighty good, young man. We'll run along now," drawled Okie Jim. "Y'all come on up to the bunkhouse if you be needing anything. Likewise, I'll be back here soon as I can in the morning."

Red took a gulp of his coffee then put a hand on Ivan's shoulder. "I'm real sorry about your Pa. He was a real good man."

Shorty put a small bottle of bootleg whiskey on the table. "You give him plenty of this. It'll ease the pain."

The men brushed past Bessie and Timmy and went out the door as cold air swept in.

Ivan set the ancestral basket beside the couch. Their father, Peter Johansen, was motionless. His face was crusted with dried mud from the tunnel where a vein of gold lured men deeper and deeper beneath the earth.

"I'll wash Papa's face," Bessie said. She peeled her beaver parka from her thin, eight-year-old body like a small bird breaking out of an eggshell. With a cloth dipped into a pan of warm water atop the wood-burning stove, she gently wiped her father's brow.

Peter Johansen opened his Aleut-Bengal-Tlingit-Swedish eyes, and they glowed proudly at the sight of his family. "My good children." he said weakly.

"Ivan got the Spirit Basket, Papa." Timmy lifted the basket in his arms with a grunt. He looked most like their mother, an Athabascan Indian with high cheekbones and strong chin.

Peter glanced at the basket then coughed. A thin

line of blood appeared at the edge of his mouth. "Take our ancestors to Attu. Take them home."

"I will, Father. You can go with me when you are well. The doctor in Fairbanks can get you well. Will you go in the dogsled tonight? The moon is full." Ivan spoke loudly sounding brave.

"Yes, my good son. Only twelve years is not very old. But, Ivan, you are a fine son who can do many things."" Peter closed his eyes.

Ivan hurriedly pulled two wolf skin rugs from the wall where they kept wind from seeping between the logs. He told Bessie to pack smoked salmon strips and pilot bread. He told Timmy to put on socks inside his warm mukluks.

"We're taking our father to the hospital." Ivan went out to hook up the dog team.

Harnessing the dogs and taking them out on a trail was something Ivan had always loved to do. But this night held no pleasure, only agony. The dogs sensed his misery. Tonight they did not bark or jump about in anticipation. All nine furry bodies patiently waited for him to fasten straps around their shoulders and down their backs. The dogs whined and held themselves in place. Ivan knotted them to the sled. One dog nudged him in a comforting way and another licked his glove.

When all the dogs were harnessed, Ivan had them pull the sled alongside the doorway. He tied them securely in place. Timmy held the lead dog's big head. Ivan and Bessie pushed their father's couch to the open door. They aligned it close to the sled.

"Father, take a drink of this whiskey so it won't hurt so much." Ivan held the sour smelling flask to Peter's quivering lips. A swallow flowed into him like it was water with no more than a blink of his tired eyes.

Ivan knew his father was too weak and injured to move himself. He had to be lifted onto the sled. There was one way he felt would work. His mother had taught him to move his arms up and down over and over before lifting a heavy object. The technique magically made a caribou body or a bear's hindquarter lightweight enough to lift up onto the cutting table.

"There is magic taught to me by Mother. We will use this magic to lift Father onto the sled."

He placed Timmy at their father's feet and Bessie at his knees. Ivan instructed them to place their hands together and raise their arms in unison with him, breathing deeply. "Up, up, up," he chanted. "Down, down. Up again. Down again. Once more." After many repetitions he commanded, "Put your hands under his feet and knees. Now lift."

Ivan lifted under his father's arms, Bessie and Timmy lifted his legs and Peter was eased onto the sled. A groan came from their father as they covered him with the fur pieces to bundle him snugly.

Bessie and Timmy curled up at their father's feet to keep his toes warm. Ivan untied the sled and mushed the dogs into a gentle trot on crisp moonlit snow.

It was the end of November and no snow had fallen for over a week, so the well used trail was hard packed. For a few moments, an aurora lighted swirls of silver that danced across the cloudless sky. The only sound was the hiss of the runners on the sled and panting of the dogs. The strong, fast dogs were as eager as ever for an outing. Ivan braked more than the dogs liked to keep at a slow, less jolting pace. Moonlit shadows rolled endlessly up the snowy mountain as he strained to see any hazard on the trail. He hoped his father would not suffer any sudden bump, nor did he want to jar Bessie or Timmy awake.

As they descended from the summit, the temperature grew noticeably colder in the valley. Ivan's black hair bristled in white threads of frost. Yet, beneath his fur parka, his body was bathed in warm moisture for he had run much of the twenty miles while holding fast to the sled. As the dogs trotted onto the frozen Chena River, lights of the town shone dimly in white ice fog. Ivan strained to see familiar landmarks in the bends of the river ice trail. Finally he spotted the bridge then the steeple of the Catholic Church. Next to the church was a two-story building. It was St. Joseph's Hospital.

Ivan's eyelashes were crusted with ice and his cheeks burned when a nun, in black dress and veil, opened the hospital door. At first she assumed he was the patient. Then Bessie and Timmy emerged from under furs on the dogsled.

"Children, come in here at once," the sturdy woman ordered.

"Our father needs the doctor. He's hurt real bad," Ivan explained.

"Father John," she called down an antiseptic-smelling hallway. "There's an injured man outside."

This brought three men, who flung on coats. As they opened the door, a billow of white fog flowed with them. The nun grabbed Ivan's arm to keep him from following. She held him firmly huddled there with his sister and brother.

Peter was brought in on a stretcher. A light bulb dangled at the end of a cord attached to the ceiling. The glare of the light shone down on a face filled with peace. No breath moved his chest. He was very still.

Everything that happened in the days that followed did not seem real to Ivan. In time he began to see more clearly. His father's body would be left in frozen storage until the summer sun thawed ground at the graveyard. Then Peter would be buried next to his wife, Tana. Ivan's mother, both her sisters and her brother, had been among the many Athabascans to die of an influenza epidemic. With none of their mother's family still living, the three of them had no relatives here.

Ivan's father had no family here because he came from a village that was very far away in Southeast Alaska. How he sailed over the ocean to Nome, then up the Yukon River and Tanana River to Fairbanks was a story Peter had told many times.

On the sixteenth day of their stay in the hospital, the priest, Father Roland, called Ivan into his office. He looked at Ivan through tortured eyes set in a pale face. He was a kind man who did not enjoy giving out bad news. "You children will need to go into an orphanage, which I'm afraid is quite far away." He spoke gently, his thick eyebrows moved curiously up and down with each word.

"We can't go to an orphanage. We can't." Ivan bolted from his chair.

"I have begun the arrangements." The priest pulled anxiously on his white collar. "You all will be better off. It is an Indian reservation in a place called Nebraska."

"No. My father wanted us to go to Attu. It is the home of many in our family."

"Well, I was not aware of that. It is a relief to

know that." His eyebrows went up in surprise. "Perhaps it would work for you to go to the coast by the new railroad. There is an Episcopal priest in Seward. He may be able to find you passage to the Aleutian Islands."

"The train?" Ivan had seen the monster train and heard it scream as it roared down an iron trail faster than a team of dogs. He knew this was the train's first winter. Just a few months old seemed very young to Ivan and he wondered how the train could possibly be strong enough to run so far at great speed.

A week later, in mid-morning winter darkness, the train gleamed with strength. When he, Bessie and Timmy stepped aboard, carrying the Spirit Basket and all they owned in a gunnysack, something stirred within Ivan. Slowly the empty sadness inside him began to wane. This big machine had the power to bring life back to his heart.

"You must be Ivan Johansen," said the Conductor. In the dim light, his beaked hat and uniform made him look very tall. "Father Roland said you wouldn't mind earning meals and fares for the three of you."

"That's right, Sir. My father always said I'm a good worker."

"I'm a good worker too," Bessie said. She clung

to a doll of moose hide that their mother had made.

"Not me," said Timmy with a pout. He wanted to stay at the nunnery where the nuns gave them care, read them stories, taught them games. Timmy knelt on a seat and pressed his face against the window.

"Ivan, when the sun gets up to the horizon, you come to the engine car. We'll show you how to stoke the boiler. That sound all right to you?" The Conductor put a hand on his shoulder.

"Yes, Sir."

"How about me?" Bessie's bright eyes of hazel color went wide.

"I'd like you to keep an eye on your little brother." The Conductor saw her face fall so he added, "I'd like this car swept out in the morning."

Bessie grinned. "I'm a good sweeper, Sir."

The Conductor left, and they settled themselves into broad, leather seats.

"What family do we have that Father Roland says is far away at a place called Attu?" Bessie pulled a fur parka off her little doll.

"When we get there, it will be only the spirits of our ancestors that we'll know."

"We can't call that our family."

"Don't worry. We are going to a good place." Ivan said to himself, '*A better place than an orphanage*'.

The train whistle sounded. Its shrillness seemed

to prickle every pore of Ivan's skin. With a jolt, steel wheels began to bump over seams in the tracks. The scream of the whistle, bumping wheels, and the chugging engine sent Timmy into Ivan's lap. His little body trembled against his brother.

Ivan held his brother, patiently explaining the noises. He anxiously watched for light to appear on the horizon so he could make his way to the engine car at the front of the train. By the time the sky filled with a pink glow, Bessie had become acquainted with other passengers and she led Timmy to a seat nearby to play with another little boy.

Ivan stepped out of the passenger car into a gust of frigid air. Frosted willow branches flashed by. As he jumped from one car over an open coupling to the next car, snowy ground rushed beneath his feet. He strode through the next car half-filled with passengers, then out again into cold air. This time he gasped. The rails were suspended high above a deep gorge. It made him dizzy to look down so he hastened into the next car.

When he reached the engine, the Engineer shouted, "This your first train trip, boy?"

Ivan nodded but didn't try to talk above the noisy engine. He soon found the job of shoveling coal into the furnace both hot and dirty. After about three hours he was told that he had helped out enough for the day. He was glad to return to sit with Bessie and

Timmy and to share wild berry jam sandwiches made by the nuns.

The train stopped for the night at Curry Station. Here a hot meal of moose stew was served in the hotel where the crew and passengers were provided beds for the night.

The next day, breakfast was sourdough pancakes before the rush to re-board was on. With a sharp whistle, the train chugged off down the track. Bessie did some sweeping and Ivan worked again in the engine room. Timmy played with his new friend. By late afternoon, the train pulled into the ocean port town of Seward.

Ivan had imagined the ocean was bigger than a lake, but not so big that he could not see the end of it. The conductor had pointed to where they could find St. Peter's Church. Carrying the Spirit Basket and bundled clothes, they stepped into a bone chilling wind that blew off Resurrection Bay. Ivan led Bessie and Timmy up a steep, snowy road to the church on top of a knoll.

They climbed the steps and stood before the door. Ivan hesitated.

"Well?" Bessie shrugged then she turned the knob and the door swung open. They stepped into the dim sanctuary.

They huddled together. Ivan was struck by how small they were next to the regal altar. Red velvet drapes hung behind a gold cross. Waxy smoke hung in the air from candles that gave off a flickering light. Their breathing was the only sound.

A door on the side of the church squeaked and a shadowy figure appeared.

"This is not a place to play," a commanding voice boomed. "You children run along now."

Timmy gasped and buried his face in Ivan's parka.

"We're not here to play, Sir," Ivan said. "We're here to see Father Rucker."

A tall, bony man walked over to them. Ivan was relieved to see that under his sweater he wore the white collar of a priest.

"We came on the railroad train," Bessie boasted.

"We go to our family," Timmy said with a voice that squeaked.

Ivan mustered his nerve and raised his voice with more confidence than he felt. "Father John Roland gave us a letter for Father Rucker."

"That would be me. Let me see the letter if you please." The priest took the letter from Ivan and held it up to a candle. He squinted as he read, glancing at them frequently with a stern frown.

"I see you are orphans," he said after finishing the letter and studying them for a moment.

"We need to get to Attu," Ivan said.

"That is a very long way, my boy." Slowly, he

looked each one of them over. "I suppose I can look into it as Father Roland suggests." Again he paused. "Meanwhile, you had better come with me."

The priest led them out the front door of the church and stopped at a house in the churchyard. Inside it was warm and smelled of roasting chicken. The priest called to his wife and introduced Mrs. Ethel Rucker, a round woman wearing an apron and a pleasant smile. She ushered them into the sitting room and insisted they take off coats and settle next to her on the sofa. Ivan remained standing.

Mrs. Rucker's eyes filled with tears when her husband read the letter aloud that told of their father dying. She hugged Bessie and Timmy tenderly. "They have come to us. It is truly a Christmas blessing."

"Ah, yes, I suppose they will be with us for a while," the solemn priest said.

She held Timmy's face in her soft hands, feasting her eyes on him. Then she did the same with Bessie. "Now don't you worry your little heads about anything. Fret about nothing but your school work, of course. Mamma Rucker is here to take care of you."

"I can read good," Bessie bragged.

"Not me," Timmy whimpered.

"Well, are you good at eating cookies and drinking cocoa?"

Ivan smiled as he watched Mrs. Rucker march his brother and sister toward a kitchen. Then he turned to the priest, whose brow was creased with deep concern.

"Father Rucker, I'm a good worker..."

"There is plenty of work here to go around, Ivan." The priest put a reassuring hand on his shoulder. "I'll be glad to have your help for as long as it takes to get you to your own people."

They were with the Ruckers for two months before the Priest announced he knew of a boat destined for Kodiak, Cold Bay and along the Aleutian Chain. He made the announcement on an evening after Bessie and Timmy were in bed.

"I won't hear of it!" Ethel Rucker cried. "Those children are a gift from God. I don't want to lose them the way we lost our little Ethan."

"Now, My Dear, the children belong with their family."

Ivan knew Mrs. Rucker was talking about a son lost to diphtheria. A girl Ivan met at church services told him the sad story.

Ivan felt it was time for him to be completely honest with these kind people. "Sir, and Mam, the truth is that it's been over a hundred years since any of our family was at Attu. Anybody we are related to there.....well, we have never met them. Not yet."

"Do you mean your little brother and sister will

be off on the dangerous sea to find only strangers in Attu?" The garment she was sewing dropped from her fingers.

"Yes, I made a promise to my father."

"Bessie and Timmy and are surely too young for such a trip," Father Rucker said.

"Well, if my brother and sister want to stay...."

"Oh yes, I'm sure they want to stay. They're much too young to go," Mrs. Rucker said. "And you're too young also, Ivan. I want you to stay here too."

"I must go!"

Ivan had turned thirteen by the time he carried the Spirit Basket to a fishing vessel bound for the turbulent waters of the Gulf of Alaska. Tears ran down Bessie's cheeks. Timmy clutched his hand.

"Your place is with the Rucker family now." Ivan gave them both a hug. "Father came to me in a dream and told me you both belong here."

"My dreams are about Papa and Mama too." Bessie sobbed.

"I like Mamma Rucker." Timmy whimpered. "But, I don't want you just in my dreams, Ivan."

Mrs. Rucker gently pulled them away to allow Ivan to board the ship. "Bessie and Timmy will say prayers for you every day."

Ivan choked out words of thanks then left them

standing on the dock. As the ship began to move Ivan was alone, yet ready to do the work of a man. He gazed out where snow-covered mountains plunged into the blue water of Resurrection Bay. Morning sunshine sparkled off silver-tipped waves. He drew in a long breath of clean, sweet sea air.

A strange mixture of excitement, calm and destiny swept through him. The unsteady deck under his feet filled him with more adventure than the runners of his dogsled or bumping steel wheels on the train.

As the journey went on and the ship was tossed about in storms, Ivan recalled the story his father told of ancestor ghosts. He suspected the foam blown off waves might have been mysterious, beckoning fingers.

One night, under a black sky sparkling with stars, he traced his hand over a red row of killer whale teeth on the basket. With certainty he knew home was near.

CHAPTER 8

THE YEAR OF 1942
The Pribilof Islands

EVACUATION

There was a knock at the door. Natasha was twelve years old on that day in June, 1942, when two American soldiers stomped in.

"The Japs are going to bomb both Pribilof Islands. People here in St. Paul and in St. George must leave immediately." A uniformed soldier tapped the butt of his rifle on the floor.

"Surely there is time for me to prepare the house and pack our things, right?" asked Ivan Johansen, Natasha's father.

"Immediate means now!" snarled a soldier with a faded green helmet pulled low on his brow. "Pack no more than one bag each. "There's no room for a bunch of junk on the *Delarof*."

The one with a riffle had a face full of worried wrinkles. "Get down to the ship before 5:00 PM. The

Japs are fixing to blow this place to smithereens like they did Attu Village."

"Where will the ship take us?" Natasha asked.

The soldiers gave no answer so she bent close to her Grandmother Eva, who did not understand the soldier's language, and whispered in the old Aleut language, "Do not be afraid."

"How long will we be gone?" asked Lukenia, her mother who tightly held the coughing baby.

The soldiers answered with shrugs. One replied, "Who knows!" Then they left to knock at the doors of other houses in St. Paul Village.

"So, the world war is coming to our island," Ivan said with a sigh.

Natasha had never heard such helplessness in her father's strong voice. He was the rock that her family depended upon. Even the whole village looked to him for guidance. He squeezed his eyes shut for a moment then shook his head.

Ivan's gentle hand patted her shoulder. "Quickly, Daughter, put your things and the baby's in the Spirit Basket." His instruction was about the precious basket he carried to Attu when he was young. There he found burial grounds for the remains of our long ago ancestors.

In the Russian language, Grandmother Eva announced, "No soldier can make me leave my home. No, I will not leave, not ever!"

Ivan answered in Russian. "The enemy soldiers have taken all the people from Attu to prison camps in Japan. This could happen here too." He gave her a brief kiss on the top of her gray hair as he passed quickly from the kitchen toward a bedroom.

Lukenia, who cuddled baby Alice in her arms, wore a frown. "Mother, we must cooperate. It is far better to go with American soldiers."

"We love you, Grandmother," Natasha pleaded in Aleut words. "Our hearts would break to leave you behind in such danger." The old woman's shoulders slumped in defeat and reluctantly she nodded her head.

In a flurry, everyone set about to gather belongings. Natasha straightened her bed, placing her Shirley Temple doll gracefully on the pillow. Its glass eyes stared happily at her. She smoothed the crocheted doily on her dresser, carefully arranged a jar of Ponds cream, a tiny perfume bottle and a wooden music box just so. She removed the hairbrush and hand mirror and bundled them in a checkered tablecloth with a couple of dresses.

"Hurry, Natasha, it is time we go," her father called.

As Natasha pulled the kitchen door closed, she glanced at the plates and cups still on the table. They had to hurry away. She wondered how this could possibly be real. Surely they would return in a few hours, or perhaps tomorrow. This was their home, the place where they belonged.

People were streaming onto the beach carrying bundles like Natasha's. Faces were filled with frowns, strain, and bewilderment. All were strangely quiet. The only voices came from soldiers shouting orders. Boats were being loaded to carry the Aleuts to an Army ship in the bay.

Ivan put a protective arm around Lukenia who she squeezed baby Alice. He said, "I will seek permission to stay a few days to prepare our home and store the bidarka."

Natasha understood that the sea-worthy bidarka was her father's means of insuring their family would be well fed with crab, shrimp and many kinds of fish.

"But if you stay here, you will be in great danger," Lukenia cried.

"If need be, there is the underground shelter and I know many hiding places. If I stay a while, I can harvest a few seals for winter. Don't worry, my love, I will catch up with you."

Ivan helped to settle Natasha's mother and grandmother into the skiff that would take them to the U. S. Army transport ship. By the time Natasha was seated, she could see her father walk up the beach toward an army officer.

A soldier pushed the skiff off. The heavily loaded boat scraped on the pebbled beach with a screech that startled Natasha, making her think of an animal in pain. All the frightened people clutched their bundles of possessions ever more tightly. Grandmother Eva's frail arms clung to a wooden egg crate filled with chinaware wrapped in cloth towels and a copper samovar (tea vessel) was tucked under her arm. These were heirlooms brought from Russia by her mother in 1860 when Alaska was still ruled by the Russian czar.

Natasha wished she had brought a tablet and pencils so she could write letters and poems. The basket, which had been woven long ago by an ancestor, was filled with important supplies and was heavy to carry.

Oars slapped into the water as two soldiers paddled the boat into the bay. The crowded skiff soon bumped against the huge ship.

"Step up quick, now," a soldier on the ship yelled. "Come on, get aboard. We ain't got all night."

Natasha fought to keep a tight hold on the spirit basket as she climbed up the unsteady boarding ladder. When she made it to the deck she turned at the rail to help her grandmother. But a long arm reached out ahead of her.

"Hey, old woman, what's that junk you're carrying?" A soldier, with a scowl on his whiskered face, grabbed the copper samovar from Grandmother Eva and tossed it into the bay. Then he yanked her aboard so roughly that the box she carried tumbled onto the deck to the sound of breaking glass.

She screamed and furiously scolded the offender in Russian words. Natasha pulled her away as quickly as she could. She managed to lead her to where Lukenia was jostling the crying baby.

Then Natasha returned to get the crate and gather up broken glass. A soldier knelt to help her. "Don't let the Sergeant get to you," he said under his breath. "He's touchy about this assignment. Thinks ships are for sailors, not dirt soldiers like us. He gets seasick." He chuckled.

"Thank you," Natasha called after him as he carried bright colored pieces of glass away.

A boy, whose eyes were as lively as a sea otter's, came up beside her. He handed her a fragile cup that was undamaged. "At least everything's not broken."

Natasha held the cup with a feeling of relief. "My grandmother will treasure this perfect cup."

More people continued to stream onto the ship's deck so the boy moved very close to her. "I am Anton from St. George Island. When we left, I thought the deck was crowded then. Wow, it's really getting mobbed now."

"I am Natasha. Thank you for helping." Natasha placed the cup in the egg crate and picked it up with trembling hands. She edged away from Anton and returned to where her family huddled together.

"Not all the china broke, Grandmother. Here is a cup that's as lovely as ever."

Her grandmother held the cup, staring at it, as if seeing it for the first time. Natasha turned away from the pain in the old, bewildered face.

Natasha caught sight of Ivan moving through the crowd. She stretched her arms up, waving them as high as she could reach. "Father! Here we are, over here," she called.

He waved back and hurried to them. "The soldiers refused to allow anyone to stay behind."

"Ivan, thank God you are coming with us." Lukenia said, cuddling the baby.

"How is Baby Alice?"

"She still coughs. I hope there is a doctor on this ship."

Natasha slipped her hand inside her father's warm grip and her trembling melted away. "A soldier was mean to Grandmother. Why is that, Father?"

"The soldiers have a big job to do. But I also do not understand their ways. They destroyed all the boats in the village."

"They treat us like dogs," Lukenia snapped.

"It's the war, my dear. Do not be bitter."

"They won't throw our spirit basket into the bay," Natasha declared. With her skirt, she covered the woven bay grass until its border of whale teeth were hidden from sight.

The *Delarof* had two decks lined with steel bunks, five bunks to a stack, designed to transport army troops. The howling Aleutian wind found its chilling way into sleeping quarters. The family spent the long days cramped together in the quarters. At mealtimes they joined long, slow-moving lines leading into the mess hall.

Official orders were so slow in coming that it was ten days before the *Delarof* finally put into a port. Over five hundred Aleuts were off-loaded at an abandoned cannery on Admiralty Island in southern Alaska.

"This place of a million trees is dark and full of strange noises," Natasha told her father as they sat on the floor of a decaying building.

"We hear a wolf howling at the moon. That is like it was in my childhood. There are trees in Interior Alaska too, though not such big ones as we see here." He retold his story of living far from the sea until he rode across Alaska in a locomotive train. Then, he told of sailing to Attu where he buried the bones of long ago ancestors. Natasha loved hearing this story.

Their home was in a building that was long, narrow and shared with many others. Each family was assigned to a ten-foot cubicle separated by hanging blankets. There was a barrel stove for heat at one end of the building but no way to heat much water so bathing and cleaning were done in cold water. The latrine was one four-hole outhouse that all the people were expected to use. Women washed clothing in a creek with a washboard. Their living conditions were far more primitive than the people had ever experienced.

"Father, when will we go home?"

"Natasha, it will depend on the Japanese who make war. I think it may be many months."

"Oh, how I wish I brought my Shirley Temple."

Her father smiled. "Your doll will be waiting for you when we return."

Lukenia frowned. "Here in this village, except for fish that is caught, there is never enough food. When there is sickness, there is no medicine. All the people need furniture, dishes and clothing."

For Natasha the worst was that there would be no school. There were only a few magazines and an occasional newspaper from Juneau, but there was no chalkboard and few pencils and paper. There was no teacher.

Her mother hugged her with sympathy. "I know you love school and want to someday be a teacher. For now, you must try to learn the things I can teach, and what your grandmother will teach."

Natasha's grandmother offered no lessons as she could only moan about the hardships. She complained about hearing the conversations of other families behind the blanket partitions. She complained about the cooking smells that filled the communal building.

Lukenia had no time to teach. All of her energy was taken with consoling the unhappy old woman and she was ever busy with little Alice.

"I think I'll be a teacher now," Natasha said one day. "I can teach the little children addition, how to write English, story-telling and songs."

With enthusiasm, she ran from one family to the next and soon she had a group of twenty students assembled. Others offered to share their knowledge too.

"I will be glad to teach everyone how to draw pictures," offered Anton Karlovich.

"I remember you, Anton. You helped me pick up my grandmother's broken china on the ship." Natasha watched him sketch on a tablet of how he remembered the *Delarof.*

Anton smiled with a light in his handsome sea otter eyes. "I remember that day. There was fear on every face."

"I wake up in the night with that memory too. I wish we could hurry and get back on that ship to take us home again."

"Things are rough here, aren't they?"

"I'm glad for some things."

"What are you glad for?" Anton slapped down a burned stick he used for charcoal drawing.

"For one thing, I like seeing you draw wonderful pictures."

"Mr. Porter asked me to draw a picture of him yesterday and he thought it looked just like him." Anton spoke of the cannery caretaker.

"Did you actually go to his big house?" Natasha swallowed with astonishment.

"I did. And it's beautiful inside, even better than any house I've ever seen. Compared to us he lives like a king."

"That's not fair." Natasha frowned, and Anton nodded in agreement.

Almost half a year later, in May, Ivan announced that he and most of the other men were recruited to harvest fur seals for use by the armed forces. Fur was needed for warm clothing.

Ivan was gone for four months, not returning until the start of their second winter. Lukenia lamented all the time he was gone and continued when he returned. "They took all you men away, leaving us with no one to repair these buildings. Then, Ivan, you return with only $19.00 earned to show for it?"

"It was our way to help with the war," Ivan replied. "The fur was needed by men fighting in faraway lands."

"I'm sad that you weren't here when Grandmother Eva got sick," Natasha said. With the palms of her hands, she wiped away tears washing over her cheeks.

Tears came to Lukenia too. "She died of a broken heart."

"Anton's little sister died of pneumonia," Natasha said. The sadness in her father's tired face made her quickly add, "But both Alice and I got over the measles just fine." She did not mention the many people who did not recover from the epidemic.

Natasha found the second winter twice as long as the one before. Tall tree branches were heavy with snow. Cloud-filled sky barely peeked through the thick forest. Space in her world seemed to close in.

Besides teaching every day, no matter what the weather, Natasha would walk along the open beach. She even braved icy winds to make sure she could see the world was not shrinking. The restless ocean reached out far, very far. Often, Anton walked with her.

"It is only out here that I feel I can breathe. There is less air in that dark forest."

Anton gave her a quizzical look then shrugged.

"Yeah, there are no trees on our islands but this is the same ocean that touches St. George and St. Paul."

"Those islands are so far away."

Finally, in the following May, good news came. After nearly two years, the *Delarof* was returning. They were finally going home. Everyone in camp gathered together and celebrated with songs. When the ship set anchor, people who boarded had the light of hope in their eyes. This time excitement filled the ship, not fear.

Together Natasha and Anton leaned into the wind on deck. "Anton, what is the first thing you will do when you reach your home on St. George Island?"

"Before we land, I will look into the cliffs to see if the spirits are welcoming us home."

Natasha looked at him suspiciously. She sometimes could not tell when he was joking.

"Well, the first thing I shall do is hug my Shirley Temple doll. Then I'll put on my Ella Fitzgerald record and lie down upon my very own bed. I will lie there listening to her sing for hours."

Anton laughed. "I hope you will get up and write a letter to a friend sometime."

"I shall write lots of letters to you." Her smile for him repeated many times, especially when the ship's first stop was at St. Paul Island and Anton was left on board.

Natasha was giddy with excitement when she lifted the spirit basket from the skiff and set her feet on the beach at St. Paul. She stood a few moments beside her father, mother and little sister as they looked around. Everything looked neglected. The Island had missed them as much as they had missed it. Natasha smiled and ran ahead. Her smile faded when she reached her home.

When her mother saw their home, she wailed, "What has become of it all? The pictures are gone from the walls, closets are empty."

Natasha spun about in her empty, dirty room. "I have no phonograph? No bureau. My Shirley Temple is gone."

Ivan ran his hand over a wall covered with dart holes and nails thick enough to hold a soldier's rifle. He scraped his foot on the ruined linoleum he had so painstakingly laid a few years ago. "The soldiers saved us from Japanese bombs, but they forgot this house was someone's home."

Natasha ran into the lamenting village where people complained about the soldiers and how they had destroyed everything including most of the caribou herd. She escaped to the top of a knoll and ran along the path above the sea wall. This was a place she had dreamed of often.

She could see and hear thousands of birds as they swooped in and out from the high cliff. Below, seals barked at one another. From here she could see and feel the whole earth. No trees loomed overhead. There was only the wide-open sky and tumbling clouds. The heaving ocean swept a fine mist freely across the hills on the wind.

"I know it is good that soldiers saved us from the evil ones." Natasha shouted to the birds and the seals and the wind. "I am home!"

CHAPTER 9

THE YEAR OF 1964
In Anchorage

EARTHQUAKE

On March 28th, 1964, at 5:36 PM, the earth beneath Alaska split open with the impact of 10,000 atomic bombs exploding. The state was struck by an earthquake rated over nine on the Richter scale.

Luke Karlovich heard a rumble coming from deep within the earth's core. He was in a motel room in Anchorage with his father Anton. An earthquake blasted the front door open.

They had experienced earthquakes before. At first, Luke smiled at the irony of the earth moving as the Bible said it had on the day Jesus died. This day was Good Friday. Yet, unlike quakes he had known on St. Paul Island, this one was lasting more than a few seconds. It went on and on.

"Luke, get outside," his father yelled. He bolted from the motel bathroom dripping wet and wrapped in a towel.

"If I can." Luke staggered into a table that slid across the floor. Linoleum under his feet buckled, throwing him into walls that billowed in. Somehow, he made it to the door that opened on it own. His father was right behind him.

In the parking lot, Luke turned back to see the building squirm, its walls tilted one way then another as if in the grip of angry spirits. Trees were swinging, cracking and toppling over in crazy patterns. Sounds were like thunder. As Anton made his way toward their rented Buick, he shouted something Luke could not hear.

Luke took a step to follow, but a black seam sliced through the snow-covered lot. He tried to back away from the widening chasm, but as if a massive hand pushed him, he tumbled forward. His face slammed nose first into the smells of salty sea and musty decaying matter. He had fallen fifteen feet into a bed of soft, soggy sand. The right side of his body was partly submerged. He felt caught in ocean waves as the earth kept rolling.

With all his strength, he tried to roll free of the burial. Wet sand weighted down his arm. He twisted and pulled until his right shoulder emerged. With his left hand he clawed at the earth and tugged on his right arm until it was free.

The rumbling earth continued to convulse beneath him. With both hands, he clawed at sand until his leg was free. Struggling to his feet, he dodged a shower of debris that rained into the crevasse. A section of the motel building loomed overhead then fell with a horrific bang, missing him by only a few feet.

Will this be the last day of my short life of fifteen years? Will the twisting earth close up, swallow me forever? Luke thought of his loving mother, Natasha, crocheting doilies to store in the spirit basket as she waited for her son and husband to come home to St. Paul Island for Easter Day.

The earth stopped moving. After a full four minutes, the rumbling and motion were gone. It was as if the earth stopped as a runner would to take a breath.

"Not my last day," Luke said aloud. He forced his trembling legs into the side of the crevasse. The caribou-hide soles of his mukluks had no grip on the wet sand and muck. His feet slipped backward. He raised his eyes up beyond the steep ridge. In the sky, billowing clouds formed the shape of strong animals resembling caribou. He exhaled deeply and repeated, "Not my last day!"

Urgently, he concentrated on the strength of a caribou until new energy flowed to his feet. With new eyes he spotted an exposed tree root inches away. He tugged, jammed his toes into the bank. One step at a time he lifted himself up, up, up. At the top he rolled onto snow.

"Dad!" he called, and frantically scanned the wreckage. The civil city of Anchorage looked like a bombed out war zone seen on TV.

In the eerie silence, a car horn sounded. Luke spotted his father waving from inside the Buick. It rested atop a piece of the street surrounded by dirt slides on all sides. It resembled the mushroom cloud of an atomic explosion. Anton opened the door and carefully eased himself out onto pavement then jumped down to unbroken ground.

At the sight of his father barefoot in the snow, wearing only a jacket from the car and clutching a damp towel around his middle, Luke laughed. Tension melted.

In turn, Anton laughed in relief. "You're a muddy mess, son. You look like you've been to the bottom of the earth."

Anton's bare feet danced through the snow to reach his son. He squeezed Luke's shoulder with his one free hand.

"I really was at the bottom of the earth." Luke still grinned at the sight of his father. "We need to find you shoes and pants, Dad."

"I don't think that'll be a problem." Anton gestured at the collapsed wall of the motel. Their room was completely exposed. Clothes were scattered about. Stunned motel guests moved about in slow motion. A relentless clang, clang, clang came from a church bell somewhere. In the distance, sirens screamed.

Anton's open suitcase was under a toppled table. He pulled out a pair of corduroys and a sweatshirt. When Anton was fully dressed, he tossed his towel to Luke. Luke found a drizzling water pipe and attempted to get washed up.

Once dressed and cleaned up, they looked blankly at one another.

"Now what, Dad?"

"I don't know. I've never seen earthquakes so destructive and that lasted so long. Maybe what we should look for people who need help."

"Or maybe dogs that need help."A beautiful malamute came toward them barking. It wasn't a threatening bark, more one of alarm. Luke grabbed her collar and gently petted her head.

"It's okay, girl."

"Sure does look like she's a nursing mother. Maybe her babies are trapped somewhere," Anton said.

The dog nuzzled against Luke. "Where are those babies of yours?"

"Luke, you go ahead and follow her. I'll be checking with people around here."

"She came from the direction of that fancy Turnagain neighborhood," Luke said.

"Get yourself back here before dark, and watch out for more quakes. There's sure to be aftershocks." Anton patted his son's back.

The dog's colorfully masked eyes focused on Luke and she uttered an urgent whine. "Come on girl, let's find those pups."

Luke followed as she began to trot away from the ruined motel. Her pace quickened, and she stopped every few yards to look back as if making sure Luke was trailing her.

Abruptly the dog ducked into a badly damaged three-car garage. Luke followed her into a darkened interior.

"Help," a whimpering voice called.

Luke could make out someone lying on the concrete floor. Within seconds, Luke was staring directly into the pale blue eyes of a boy he hated.

The dog licked the face of the boy who Luke had once heard others call Rusty.

They stared at one another. The memory of the day before burned between them. Rusty and two others had taunted Luke as they sped past him on their bikes. One bike aimed directly at Luke then swerved in time to barely miss him.

"Nice move, Rusty," one of them had snickered.

"Out of the way, Native," Rusty had shouted and gave him 'the finger'. They all laughed with their heads thrown back. Their message was clear. Being an Alaska Native somehow made Luke not their equal.

The incident had confused and shaken Luke. It had been an unsettling week for him. He had never been away from home before and was excited to be in Alaska's biggest city where 48,000 people lived. He was proud of his father for coming to Anchorage to fight for Native land rights. It had been a battle that began in 1959 when President Dwight Eisenhower declared Alaska no longer a United States territory. As the 49th state, Alaskans would elect governors and have U.S. Representatives who could vote to make and change laws.

Yesterday, after the bicycle threat, Luke longed for the week to end so he could go home to his island where there were no people like Rusty.

"Shemya, good girl," Rusty gasped. His frightened eyes shifted to Luke. "You got to go get me some help, man."

Rusty lay trapped by collapsed garage wall. A log beam pinned him to the floor. Blood flowed from a gash in his leg.

"Don't try to move. An aftershock could come any second," Luke said. "It's not likely you have time for firemen to show up."

One end of the beam, that had Rusty pinned, rested on an unstable pile of debris. The slightest movement could send the beam full-force onto his neck.

Luke looked about until he found a plank to wedge beneath the beam just above Rusty's head. He worked it carefully in place.

"Come here, Shemya, over here," Luke called to the dog to get her out of the way. The dog was well trained and responded without hesitation.

Then Luke fell onto the plank with all his weight.

"Roll!" he shouted.

Rusty slid clear of the beam.

"How did you know to do that? How did you know…? Thanks. Thanks," Rusty gasped, his whole body shaking.

"That leg looks bad." Luke sounded as calm as a sergeant in charge.

"The pups. I got to find my dog's pups." Rusty's voice trembled with each shaky word.

"Hold still. A bandage may stop the bleeding." Luke retrieved a pillow that had mysteriously flown to the garage floor from a bed that was nowhere in sight. He yanked off the pillowcase, opened a blade on his pocketknife and slashed it into bandage strips.

Luke tied the cloth tightly around Rusty's wound. It pulled gashed flesh together, obstructing the flow of blood. By the time the leg was bandaged, Shemya had disappeared.

"She's gone to her pups." Rusty struggled to his

feet. He put out his hand to Luke. "Name is Rusty Smith."

Luke took the trembling hand and looked squarely into somber blue eyes. "I'm Luke Karlovich from St. Paul Island."

"I owe you, man. I know I was a real jerk yesterday when......"

A hard jolt stopped Rusty. An aftershock made wood crack with the sound of a rifle shot. Glass shattered. He stumbled and fell in a sprawl to the floor.

Luke rode out the quaking earth standing on sea legs used to motion.

"That was a sharp one." Luke grasped Rusty's hands and pulled him to his feet.

"Yeah, it was scary. But, if you hadn't gotten me out from under that beam..." Rusty quickly wiped away tears that splashed down freckled cheeks.

Luke winced and looked away, not feeling ready for Rusty's gratitude. "Okay, where are those pups?"

"In the basement. Hope we can get there." Limping, Rusty led the way down wide, sturdy stairs. Part of an upper floor had crashed through the ceiling creating an obstacle course. They edged their way down stairs to the basement floor. Rusty flipped a light switch but no lights came on. Shemya barked.

"She's by my game room. Oh no, the door is jammed by the freezer."

Luke saw a chest freezer was so lodged that the mother dog couldn't reach her pups. "If we clear some of this stuff out of the way, I think we can move it."

"Yeah, let's try."

Shemya continued to bark to let her puppies know she was nearby. In fading light that filtered from high windows, Rusty pet her and moved slowly with his stiff, painful leg. Luke moved objects blocking the freezer including a toppled television, phonograph records in bright LP covers, a lava lamp with green blobs, and a sea of comics with torn covers. Rusty helped push on the freezer until the doorway was cleared.

"Shemya girl, your pups are okay." Rusty slid to the floor and four pups climbed onto his lap.

"Those are great dogs, as fine as any sled dogs I ever saw," Luke said.

"Thanks for helping me get to them. Man, I couldn't do it without you."

Uneasy about being praised by Rusty, Luke glanced around. "Anyone else in your house?"

"My dad's away on a business trip and Mom went shopping. I sure hope she's safe." Worried lines filled Rusty's face. "Boy, will she freak out when she sees the house."

"At least, it looks like part of your house is livable." Luke noticed walls above them stood straight enough.

"Well, maybe. Want to take the dogs and go check it out with me?" Rusty sounded like he was talking to an old friend.

Luke hesitated, then shrugged and picked up a couple pups. With squirming pups under their arms, Shemya led the way up stairs.

It was the biggest house Luke had ever been in. They went from room to room, stepping over smashed glassware, fallen books and framed pictures. As they made their way to the kitchen, Luke answered questions about why he had come to Anchorage from St Paul Island.

"Wow, the Pribilof Islands!" Excitement came into Rusty's eyes. "I hear the fur seals come in there by the thousands. If I can talk my dad into going out there this summer, could you show me?"

Rusty set down his pups and brushed spilled flour off a bunch of bananas. He tossed one to Luke, who caught it while juggling two pups.

"Sure. It's a sight to see." Luke smiled.

A car door slammed and Shemya barked.

"Rusty, Rusty. Are you here?" a woman's panicky voice called.

"Yeah, Mom."

A visibly shaken blonde woman rushed into the kitchen and threw her arms around her son.

"Thank God you're all right. I thought I would

never get here. The streets are broken up; buildings are down. And this house, look at our house! I was so worried about you."

"Mom, this is Luke Karlovich." Rusty backed away from his mother's embarrassing kisses. "Luke helped me out. My leg was bleeding and the pups were trapped."

She grasped Luke's hand in both of hers and one of the pups slipped to the floor. Gratitude poured from her with praise for bandaging the leg and helping Rusty with the dogs. She thanked him over and over.

It was Luke's turn to feel embarrassed. "I had better go see how my father's doing."

Mrs. Smith wished him well then disappeared to explore the wreckage of her living room and beyond.

"Luke." Rusty put a hand on his arm. "I want you to have the pick of the litter."

"But….I can't. I mean these dogs are the greatest…"

"I mean it, man." Rusty's eyes went teary. He lowered his voice so his mother would not hear. "You saved my life."

Luke hesitated, so taken aback he did not know what to say. Just then the pup he held gave him a lick across his cheek.

Rusty chuckled. "Looks like the choice is made. He's the biggest and strongest in the litter."

Luke cuddled the furry, warm and wiggling body. "This pup is terrific."

"Okay, Luke, what are your going to call him?"

Luke's face lit up with a grin. "His name is Easter. That's because something good happened out of this Good Friday quake."

They both laughed.

Luke and Easter went out into the torn street. The snow on the towering Chugach Mountains was turning to shades of pink and purple in the setting sun, like every other March evening throughout the ages. However, this was a day unlike any other. This day would be remembered in history.

The flaming sky glistened over the Inlet water, and Luke could see faces of hope in the billowing clouds. As he ran his fingers over the pup's little head with its bright, trusting eyes, a strong certainty washed over him. He knew the people here had the spirit to rebuild the city. Maybe even a better city.

Luke peeled the banana Rusty had given him. Thoughts of all that had happened spun dizzily through his head. His visit to the big city had shaken him in ways that would stay with him throughout his whole life.

CHAPTER 10

THE YEAR OF 1989
Valdez

THE SPILL

    To conclude her class project, Deborah said, "My grandmother helped get an apology and payment to the people for being treated unfairly." Her eighth grade teacher, Mr. McGee, thanked Grandmother Natasha. Everyone clapped.

    Deborah beamed at her grandmother from St. Paul Island, who was visiting Valdez after a trip to Washington D.C. For Deborah's school project, she persuaded her grandmother to tell the class why she flew there to give testimony to the United States Congress. Grandma Natasha told Congress how in World War II, Native Alaskans were taken from the Aleutian Islands to camps that were safe from Japanese attack. After two years in poor living conditions, they were returned to damaged homes and destroyed property.

When school was out, Deborah and her grandmother walked on the road blanketed with snow and up a path toward home. "Everyone in my class was really surprised that the soldiers did not respect homes in villages."

"You will find that some people come to Alaska to take, only to take. Our people must always work to protect the land."

"Grandmother, I love when you come to visit." Deborah gave a quick kiss to her cheek.

Near her home nestled at the foot of a mountain, dogs in the kennel began to bark. "Your dogs sound like a beach full of fur seals," Grandmother Natasha said with a chuckle. "You love to hook those big malamutes to a sled and race off on a trail, don't you, my dear?"

"Oh yes, Grandmother. They're strong and fast, just like Dad's old dog, Easter."

"Your father loved that dog. I'm sure he told you many times about how he brought Easter home after that huge earthquake many years ago. The dog was a gift from a boy whose life he saved."

"Easter was a champion racer, and so is his grandson. My leader, Adak, has led me to win trophies."

When they entered the house, the scent of wild raspberry pie greeted them and so did toddler, Dee Dee. Deborah picked up her little cousin who was being cared for today by her mother, Ruth.

"Doggies go, go," the toddler said as Deborah pulled off snow-caked sneakers.

"Please do take your little cousin with you when you exercise your dogs." Ruth sat pumping a treadle sewing machine. Even though they had electricity, her mother preferred the machine she grew up using in her Yupik village far to the north. She was sewing a parka for a customer who ordered it with beautiful fur trim.

Deborah took a mink pelt out of Dee Dee's tiny hand and peered into her bright brown eyes. "Do you want to ride in the dogsled?"

The little girl squealed with delight.

Deborah grabbed a cookie, told Dee Dee she would be right back, and rushed out to get the dogs hooked up. When that was done, her grandmother had the little one outfitted in a snowsuit and ready to be bundled into the sled.

Lead dog Adak and four others filled the crisp, snow-scented air with a concerto of eager barks. They tugged eagerly and exhaled puffs of white steaming breath. Until she had Dee Dee loaded and was completely ready, Deborah held the impatient dogs back. Then she stepped onto the runners, dropped the rope that tied down the sled, and released the brake.

The dogs charged onto the trail. They pulled

hard on soft snow at a fairly slow pace that was pleasing since her favorite little passenger was aboard. She chose the trail along the bay toward the Old Valdez abandoned town site devastated by the earthquake and tsunami twenty-five years ago. An old pier nearby was usually a good place to spot sea otters at play.

Deborah stopped the dogsled whenever there was a sea otter or flocks of birds for the toddler to see and talk about. Before they headed back home, she took a trail south toward the oil company terminal.

The Trans-Alaska Oil Pipeline ran 800 miles from the Arctic Ocean, through the Interior, and ended at the ice free Bay of Valdez. In the shadow of towering mountains, an oil tanker docked there looked immense. The name on the side read, *The Exxon Valdez*, and it was said to be longer than three football fields, as tall as a twelve-story building.

As the sled dogs pulled them back home, Deborah's thoughts were on the ominous giant ship. But on this day, she did not know it would become infamous, an object of disaster.

The next morning was Good Friday, March 24th, and the radio was on. Deborah, her father, mother and grandmother sat over breakfast bowls of warm oatmeal topped with last summer's wild blueberries taken from the freezer. The radio announcer had shocking news.

Deborah's father, Luke, turned up the volume to hear a recorded voice from the oil tanker *Exxon Valdez*. It was the voice of Captain Hazelwood, "We've fetched up hard aground, leaking some oil."

Luke slammed down his cup. Coffee splashed onto the table. The news commentator went on to explain. "Shortly after midnight, the oil tanker crashed into Bligh Reef, just 23 miles out of Valdez. Untold thousands of gallons of crude oil are spilling into Prince William Sound."

Luke jumped up from the table.

The radio voice said, "Fishermen in the area are called for an emergency meeting at the Valdez Café."

"I'd better get down to the waterfront." Luke pulled his coat from a peg near the door.

"It sounds terrible!" Deborah gasped, her stomach tightened. Breakfast was forgotten.

Luke turned back and reached for the ringing phone. "Hello, this is Luke Karlovich. I heard about it. Now it sounds like the herring season could close."

Hearing those words made Ruth moan, "Oh no, how will we manage if we miss a whole season?"

Tears came to Grandmother Natasha. "Oil on the water in the Sound? Oil washing onto the shores?" Deborah put her arms around her grandmother as they listened to Luke talk to another fisherman.

"Just last night at the fisheries meeting, Riki was right when she warned us that this could happen someday," Luke said of a local biologist. "Well, it looks like that day is here. I'll see you at the café." When he hung up, he headed for the door.

"Dad, I want to go with you. I can go to school from the cafe." Deborah grabbed her coat and followed him outdoors where dogs yelped.

"You mutts quiet down. Hush up, Adak," Deborah called. "I fed them already this morning," she assured her father as they climbed into his pickup.

Snow was plowed in banks along the street, over-hanging pine boughs were crusted with frost. Luke stopped the pickup with a jolt. The cafe parking lot was nearly full.

"It looks like everyone in town is here," Deborah said. Her sneakers squished in spring mud and slush as she followed her father into the building.

The café rang with loud voices. Faces wore bitter frowns. Men talked all at once. They cursed the oil company and accused the ship's captain of being drunk.

A burly man with a Swedish accent banged his fist on a table with such force that everyone listened. "For over seven hours oil has been pouring out into the sound. So far the oil companies have done nothing to stop or contain it."

"Right, Jeb, and don't we know where that oil is headed?" warned a man with grey hair and sun reddened cheeks. "It might flow straight at the fish hatchery."

A young Native man shook his head. "Most of the containment gear at the oil marine terminal is buried under four feet of snow. That crew will be a week getting ready to do anything."

Luke's big hands held a steaming coffee cup. After listening intently, he spoke up. "No one cares about the Sound the way we do. We can't wait around for corporate presidents to figure out what to do to save that hatchery. If it gets saved, we will have to do it."

Deborah looked from one tough man's agitated face to the next. A thick fog of silence fell over the room until her innocent voice rang out. "Dad, couldn't we string a giant net across the spill to keep the oil out of the bay?"

Snickers and indulgent grins went around the room.

Luke's dark eyes lit up like a spark. With his calloused seaman's hands on Deborah's shoulder, he said, "She makes me think we just might. Instead of a net, if we can get enough containment boom to float, it will be worth a try."

Men nodded but looked doubtful. One asked, "Where in the world could we ever come up with that much boom?"

"Sweden," Jeb said. "I can get it flown here in a couple of days."

Luke gave him a nod. "If this weather holds, that might be soon enough."

"We could start a skimming operation too," said a fisherman from Cordova, the nearest port to the south. He talked with his arms waving around to demonstrate how oil could be slopped into herring roe cans.

Deborah left the meeting and ran the few blocks to the school. Before entering the building, she looked back at blue water in the bay with hordes of white birds circling above. There was no sign of the tragedy here, except in the faces of people.

In her classroom, no one talked of anything but oil flowing from the tanker into bays that were too far away to see.

"Will the icky oil come into our harbor?" a student asked with her nose crinkled.

"It's not likely," Mr. McGee replied. On the blackboard the eighth-grade teacher drew a sketch of Prince William Sound. He put an 'X' on a spot to mark Bligh Reef. "This is where the spill is. From there the current is more likely to carry the oil south and west. It could also move along the coast for hundreds of miles."

"What will happen to seals and otters if they get covered with oil?" Deborah asked. In that moment she thought of all the animals that swim in the sea.

"I think the oil could even kill whales," a boy said.

"What about birds that land in the water?" another boy asked.

"Fish and Wildlife Services will need a lot of help to try to clean birds and animals," Mr. McGee said.

"I want to help!" Deborah cried, and the rest of the class chimed in.

"Good, I'll look into it as soon as the animal hospital is setting up."

At dawn, on the third day after the spill, Deborah begged her father to let her ride out to the oil spill with him and the crew. "I can make sandwiches and coffee for you."

"It'll be dark before we get back, but your help would be good." Luke gave his daughter a hug.

Luke's boat, the St. Paul Clipper, and a flotilla of other fishing boats set out on the calm waters of Valdez Bay and through the narrows. They chugged pass Sawmill Bay and Jack Bay that peacefully reflected towering mountains in glass-smooth waters. Beyond Galena Bay, other fishing boats from Cordova were at work setting oil-containment booms.

Bligh Reef and the immense *Exxon Valdez* tanker came into sight. A smaller tanker was in place to pump oil from the damaged ship. Streaking out from the tanker toward Columbia Glacier Bay was an enormous oil slick. Icebergs that broke off the glacier floated out to sea wearing ugly black oil skirts. A massive, top-heavy iceberg rolled over and looked like it turned into a glossy, black floating boulder.

The air was scented with the stench of crude oil. Deborah swore her tongue could taste the fumes. She moved cautiously about the boat to stay out of the way of her father and three-man crew. They wrestled with a massive pile of boom. Men shouted from the decks of a dozen boats to coordinate the effort.

After hours of intense labor, Luke trudged into the galley for a break.

"How is it going, Dad?"

"So far, it seems to be working. San Juan hatchery just might get saved." He took off his knit hat and ran a hand through his short-cut hair that was wet with sweat.

Deborah poured coffee into a tin cup and handed it to him. "I keep seeing birds fly over. I hope none will land in the oil."

"Unfortunately, they don't know the danger."

Those words were no sooner spoken, when out the portside window, she saw a cormorant alight directly onto a thick flow of oil. Deborah ran up on deck. With its beak the bird scraped at oil on its body. It fluttered its wings, which coated them more and more with black goo. The oiled wings would not fly. Minutes later, its body lay motionless on the oil slick.

With eyes that stung from petroleum fumes and tears, Deborah watched murres, kittiwakes and an eagle meet the same fate. Before the day was out, a marbled murrelet flapped close to the boat. Luke leaned over the side with a net and brought the bird aboard.

As it lay in a gooey puddle, Deborah hurriedly wiped the bird with paper towels. It should have fought like the wild thing it was, but it listlessly submitted. Deborah could feel its terrified heart beating rapidly. It made weak attempts to flap gummy, oil-coated wings and gave off a raspy squawk. Then it went limp and she could no longer feel a heartbeat.

Deborah turned to her father. "Did the oil kill it or did it die of fright?" Neither he nor a crewman answered. They looked away to the open sea with pain in their eyes.

In the days that followed, the obscure community of Valdez was part of the nation's daily news. Television cameras focused on beaches strewn with dead and dying seabirds. There were seals and sea otters, too, their big eyes bewildered by the suffocating oil that left them sick and immobile. Biologist put them into cages to be transported to care centers where a bath might save them.

Outrage felt in Valdez was shared across America and around the world. The unthinkable had happened in Alaska's pristine waters. Eleven million gallons of oil had spilled.

Thousands of people crowded into the tiny town. Politicians came, including United States Vice President Quayle. People from state and federal agencies and from other nations came to try to save animals and birds. Many more were there to wipe oil off rocks on rugged shorelines. Everyone, including Deborah's class, protested against the oil companies for the broken promise. The companies had claimed to be prepared for a catastrophe, but they were not.

One evening Grandmother Natasha said, "It's time for me to go back to St. Paul Island to be with your grandfather, Anton."

"I wish you would stay longer," Deborah sighed. She put her head on her grandmother's lap. Her muscles ached from hours of helping at the animal hospital. Her heart ached even more from seeing animals and birds die because, in spite of all the hard work, very few were saved. She wondered if the stench of the thick crude oil would be with her forever.

"You know I love to be with you, my children, but here I feel closed in by all these tall mountains, trees and glaciers."

Deborah smiled. She knew Grandmother Natasha would never be convinced that any place was home except the treeless Pribilof Islands.

"Thank you for bringing the spirit basket, Grandmother. I promise to give it care and keep it safe." Deborah said. "It is good to have it there on a shelf because it has so many stories to tell."

The old basket was the yellow color of winter grass. It was woven with a design of faded red orca teeth around its full body.

"I leave the basket here to bring you strength. It has seen many hard times, harder even than the spill of oil. Yet, the basket and our people survive."

"I will always remember that, Grandmother." For the first time since the oil spill, Deborah thought about stories from long ago years. With her hands on the basket, she remembered how people had bravely faced challenges and fought hard to earn better lives for their children and grandchildren.

Hope came back into Deborah's heart.

CHAPTER 11

THE YEAR OF 2015
Fairbanks

NATIVE OLYMPIC GAMES

My heart is thumping in my ears. My hands are slick with sweat and I'm not even on stage yet. In Alaska, the Indian-Eskimo Olympic Games are held every year. To demonstrate what the games and dances are about, the Museum of the North will put on a daily show this summer. Today is my first time ever to perform for an audience of strangers.

A crowd of mostly white-haired tourists should be enough to make me nervous, but that's not it. My sweat is caused by two teenagers in the crowd. They are the last two in the long line outside the theater door. They've got me in full-blown stage fright.

Yesterday, those same two guys passed me on skateboards in a mall parking lot. Then they loomed up in front of me again when I wandered into the Music Man Shop. Like Hollywood teens on TV, they were dressed alike. Shiny studs sparkled from eyebrows and earlobes. Bare arms were covered in tattoos. Flowered pants billowed out, truly baggy. The tank top on the taller one had orange stripes, the other guy's was a florescent green that echoed streaks in his blond hair.

The shorter one examined a CD, his expression betraying nothing. The other responded with a grunt, and they headed for the checkout counter. When they were gone, I bought the same CD even though I'd never heard of the Pizzollas. When I got a chance to play it, I found it real cool.

Now, they are here in our audience looking as mod as ever. I slither behind the show poster board that's just big enough to hide my costume of fringed caribou skin and is trimmed with beads.

"Jared!" My cousin Dee Dee calls from a table where she's signing autographs. Dee Dee is a dog musher and was the one who talked me into all this. She begged me to do it. But, she really didn't have to overdo it. There isn't much I wouldn't do if she asked. When I was a little kid, Dee Dee was there for me. She took care of me like her favorite puppy whenever asked by my mother, Deborah. In a way, Mom was her teacher for training dogs and full of tips on how to race them.

So what else could I say when she showered me with praise? For at least 60 seconds she had me believing I was the only creature on land who could interpret the dance of whaling. I agreed to come to Fairbanks mostly because she said she needed me. That was the biggest compliment. She's the director of the show.

"Bring me some more pictures, will you Jared?" Dee Dee calls.

I scoot out from behind the sign. In the closet-sized storeroom I find the box marked "Dee Dee Karlovich" and take out a stack of the pictures. They're of her and her dog team crossing the finish of the Iditarod race in Nome last March. Dee Dee didn't win the 1200-mile race from Anchorage to Nome, but she finished in less than eleven days. That put her in the top five. She and her dogs had cleverly outrun many of the 62 other mushers.

For over a week back then, my ear had been glued to the radio for the news from the Nome finish line. It was nearly midnight when her name was announced as a finisher. I was hoarse from yelling, you'd have thought I was the one with my face in the stinging wind that blew off the Bering Sea. The next day at school, I made myself absolutely obnoxious by bragging to everyone.

Performing in these games isn't the only reason I left St. George Island for the summer. Dee Dee also needs help with her 32 dogs. Then there is the matter of the spirit basket. My great grandmother insisted I bring our ancestral basket to the Museum of the North.

Rhythm being beat out on drums breaks into my daydream. The show is beginning. I hustle out to Dee Dee's table with the photos.

"That sounds like your cue," she says with a brilliant smile. "I'll catch your act in a few minutes. Hurry now."

The line is gone so that means everyone is seated in the auditorium. I glance out the huge windows that look down upon the green Tanana River Valley and beyond at the distant snow-covered Alaska Mountain Range.

I slip through the side door and am immediately on stage with the others. The stage seems a whole lot smaller than it had at practice. The audience is right there. I mean only a few feet from the risers. The heads in the front row are either white-haired or little kids'. They're all smiling, unthreatening. Such a bright spotlight hits my eyes that I can't see into the darker rows. I begin to relax.

Introductions are in progress. There are seven of us, three university students and the rest of us are high-schoolers. Brad, who is from Shishmaref is giving his family history to the audience. I am next. I'd practiced the words written by Dee Dee at least a hundred times. "Speak slowly, be loud and clear and be sure to smile," she had coached.

"My name is Jared Sheikov. I'm from St. George in the Pribilof Islands. My family moved there from Valdez after the 1989 oil spill ruined fishing in Prince William Sound. My ancestors lived off the land and sea in Alaska all the way from the Aleutians to Nome. My heritage is mostly Aleut, but a Swede, a couple of Russians, a Tlingit, an Eskimo and an Athabascan Indian are part of my ancestry too." There are some chuckles.

"On St. George Island we practice games of skill to sharpen our hunting skills, and we celebrate with song and dance." My cheeks are burning fire at the end of my speech, but people applaud so I guess I said it okay.

The games begin with Samuel and Brad competing in the two-footer kick. They astonish the crowd by jumping up and tapping their feet on a sealskin ball that dangles a couple of feet above their heads. Both land squarely on their feet.

Matthew and I demonstrate the one-foot high kick. My legs feel tight and I charge too fast on the first try, but on the second try I tap the ball. Next I do the greased-stick pull with Lucy, a really cute Inuit Eskimo from Point Hope. She has sparkling eyes and a smile that makes me feel happy all over. The audience "ooh" and "ah" at our athletics and shower us with applause.

I join in the Inupiaq dance that we had practiced daily for two weeks. Matthew and Samuel beat hide drums with sticks. Brad plays the part of a walrus being hunted. With Lucy beside me, we pursue the walrus and show the story by motioning with feathered fans and rhythmic steps. We also sing in Yupik. I fake some of the words that are all new to me. Again, there is plenty of applause.

Dee Dee knows how to make sure the audience has fun. When we demonstrate how to twirl the seal skin balls of the Eskimo yo-yo, she invites people from the audience to come onto the stage and participate. The first one up on stage is the teen with green streaks in his blond hair. He is the one I had seen at a music counter and hid from today.

As if he's royalty, Dee Dee beams at him. "Tell us your name and where you're from." She shoves a microphone before to his mouth.

"I'm Derek from L.A." He holds out his arm decorated with tattoos and shakes Dee Dee's hand like a gentleman.

"Jared will show you, Derek." Dee Dee turns away to invite someone else to the stage.

It doesn't even occur to me that I should cringe or run away. Maybe all that applause gave me courage. Besides, this guy is on my turf now. I hand him a yo-yo.

"Start the motion up and down, like this," I say while flipping a string. "Then toss one ball in a circle this way. Get it going and toss the other in an opposite circle."

"Like this?" Derek's yo-yo makes a couple of passes then the balls bang together and fall limp.

"Try again. Keep your hand going up and down. That's the way." I relish being a coach.

"Yeah, Man, this needs a bunch of practice. It'd be so cool if I get the yo-yo hang before flying south."

"No problem. You'll catch on." I'm beginning to think I've got a knack for this. Maybe I'll pursue a teaching career.

The drums begin with a hollow beat, beat, beat. The people return to their seats. I take center stage and start the dance of whaling. This dance ends the performance. The audience jump to their feet with enthusiastic applause.

We leave by the side door and hurry around to the entrance. We form a line to greet the people as they exit the theater.

Derek passes by with his friend. "Thanks for the tips, Jared. I'm getting a yo-yo to take back to L.A."

The friend's studded eyebrows sparkle in sunlight coming from the windows. He holds up a high-five hand and mumbles, "Real cool show, Man."

All I do is grin at them as they amble toward the

Museum gift shop. I utter the standard, "Thanks for coming. Enjoy Alaska."

An old man grasps my hand, shaking it like the handle of a well pump. His wife tells me to always be proud of my Native heritage. Someone else calls me an athlete. Another insists I keep my people's traditions alive.

"Well, how was it?" Dee Dee beams at me.

"Better than I thought." The truth is that I felt like I'd just hit a home run in a World Series.

"Let's go call Grandma and tell her all about it."

"Wait, Dee Dee, maybe we shouldn't call. You know Great Grandma Natasha will ask about the basket." Dr. Lee had not promised a spot to display the ancestor basket.

"Didn't I tell you?" Dee Dee gives me a teasing grin. "Come on."

I follow her through the Gallery passing the giant Kodiak bear named Otto. We pass the mammoth tusks, the oomiak, polar bear and enter the Southwest Alaska exhibit. There, in a case with other handmade items is the spirit basket. Beside it is a message that I read aloud. "Circa 1800. Basket is made from bay grasses grown in the Aleutian Islands and Kodiak Island. Orca tooth traditional design colored Red from local berries."

My throat is tight and my eyes sting a little as we gaze at the old basket. It strikes me that it looks a little like it's entombed behind glass.

"It feels like two hundred seventy years of stories are trapped in there. What will happen to the stories?"

Dee Dee smiles. "The stories live in our hearts. They are ours to tell."

I begin to feel a magical calm.

"That's cool!" I say.

THE END

ALASKA BACKGROUND INFORMATION

Aleut: Native people principally in the Aleutian Chain Islands.

Basket Weaving: Natural resources used by Alaska Native people for making containers for gathering, storing and cooking. Depending upon the location, materials included beach grass, birch or cedar bark, spruce root or baleen. Beach grass was the primary material used to make baskets by Aleut people.

Aleut Gut Parka – Kamleika: A coat made from the intestines of sea mammals. Seams of sinew would swell when wet making the parka waterproof. Kamleika is a Russian word.

Labret: A Russian word for a carved piece of bone, ivory, wood or stone worn in a perforation in the lower lip or cheek. It is held in place by a flared retainer that is carved out.

Bidarka: An Aleut skin boat.

Tlingit: Natives, language, and area inhabited by people in Southeast Alaska, particularly in the Sitka area.

Potlatch: A celebration with food and dance.

Aleksandr Baranov: First Chief Manager of Alaska for the Russian America Company, 1790 to 1818. Established colonies and became Governor of Russian America.

Father Ioann Veniaminov: A priest and bishop for the Russian Orthodox faith, who developed an alphabet and scriptures in native languages and was skilled in crafts, carpentry and sciences.

Purchase of Alaska: In 1867 the Czar of Russia agreed to sell the territory of Alaska for 7.2 million dollars (about 2-cents an acre), money needed to finance wars in Russia.

Seward's Folly: A term used in many newspapers (also Seward's Icebox) to describe the purchase of Alaska as a waste of money at the time the U.S. was recovering from the Civil War. The purchase was negotiated with Russia by William H. Seward, who served as Secretary of State for President Abraham Lincoln and President Andrew Johnson.

Ceremonial Robes: When wool blankets from the Hudson Bay Company began to be traded to Native people in southeast Alaska in the 1800's, they often made them into robes for celebrations. They decorated the robes with bone, shells and, eventually with buttons that outlined a clan's traditional design or crest.

Alaska Gold Rush: People rushed to Juneau when gold was discovered in 1880. In 1893 they rushed to Birch Creek near Circle City. Dawson City in the Yukon Territory began when gold was found in 1896. Another gold rush caused the founding of Nome in 1898. Felix Pedro staked a claim in the hills of the Tanana Valley in 1902 and gold rushers built the town of Fairbanks.

Bedrock Gold Mining: A shaft is drilled 14 to 100 feet below the surface to lift out rock in a vein of gold. Loads of rocks are gathered from miles of tunnel.

Sluicebox: Rock and dirt are dumped into troths and flooded with water. As water runs, rock and dirt wash away leaving gold flakes and nuggets to cling on the bottom surface.

Athabascan: Indian people who settled in the interior of Alaska.

Alaska Railroad: Railroad runs 470 miles from Seward to Fairbanks. President Warren G. Harding drove a golden spike at Nenana signifying completion in July 1923. The tracks reached Fairbanks in 1925, connecting the town with ports at Anchorage and Seward.

Aleut Evacuations in WWII: In 1942 the Japanese bombed and invaded Attu and Kiska in the Aleutians. For safety, the military evacuated villages in the Aleutians and Pribilof Islands. Families were evacuated 800 miles to the southeast at old canneries with few supplies. In 1988 U. S. Congress granted $12,000 to survivors to compensate for property losses.

1964 Earthquake: The 9.2 magnitude quake occurred on March 28, 1964 at 5:36 P.M. local time. It lasted four minutes and was centered near Valdez. Damage occurred from massive landslides, fractures and tsunamis in Alaska waters and beyond. 115 people died in Alaska. Twelve were killed by seismic waves in Crescent City, California, and four in Newport Beach, Oregon.

Exxon-Valdez Oil Spill: On March 23, 1989 the oil tanker Exxon-Valdez left the port of Valdez with a full load of crude oil. Just after midnight, the tanker ran onto Blyth Reef. Eleven million gallons of oil poured from eight-foot holes into the sea.

Oil Spill Charges: The Exxon-Valdez ship captain Joe Hazelwood was charged and fined $59,000 plus 1,000 hours to scrub oily rocks on the shore. Exxon was fined $125 million for a penalty and over $500 million in compensation to citizens.

World Indian-Eskimo Olympics: A competition held annually in Alaska. Participants represent Native villages in Alaska, Yukon Territory, and Northwest Territory in Canada. Games evolved in Native cultures to promote development of physical skills for hunting and fishing. Dances and songs celebrate history and stories of the people.

Resource References:

Alaska, A History of the 49th State, Second Edition, Claus-M. Naske and Herman E. Slotnick, University of Oklahoma Press, Norman, Oklahoma.

Sharing Alaska Native Cultures, A Hands-on Activity Book, Project Director - Terry Dickey, University of Alaska Museum of the North, Fairbanks, Alaska.

Crooked Past, The History of a Frontier Mining Camp: Fairbanks, Alaska, Terrence Cole, University of Alaska Press, Fairbanks, Alaska.

Trail of Tears Forges Strong Woman, Judy Ferguson, Heartland, Fairbanks Daily News Miner, October 31, 2004 edition, Fairbanks, Alaska.

Fairbanks, A Pictorial History, Claus-M. Naske and Ludwig J. Rowinski, The Donning Company, Norfolk, Virginia.

Forced to Leave, Exhibit at University of Alaska Museum of the North, Ronald K. Inouye, curator, Wanda W. Chin, exhibit coordinator.

Exxon Valdez, Legacy of a Spill, A Special Section of the Anchorage Daily News, March 21, 1999, Anchorage, Alaska.

Fairbanks Daily News-Miner articles printed the 24th, 25th and 26th of March, 1964 concerning the Exxon Valdez oil spill, Fairbanks, Alaska.

Looking North, Art from the University of Alaska Museum, Edited by Aldona Jonaitis, University of Washington Press.

Lost Heritage of Alaska, The Adventures and Art of the Alaskan Coastal Indians, Polly and Leon Gordon Miller, Bonanza Books, New York, NY, 1967.

Russian America, The Great Alaskan Venture 1741-1867, Hector Chevigny, Binford & Mort, Thomas Binford, Publisher, Portland, Oregon.

ABOUT THE AUTHOR

Marie Osburn Reid has enjoyed watching changes take place in Alaska since it became a state in 1959. She moved from Truckee, California to the "Land of the Midnight Sun" in 1958. With her first husband, Austin G. Ward, they raised three children in Fairbanks.

Her greatest inspirations for THE SPIRIT BASKET were outstanding collections and displays at the University of Alaska Museum of the North in Fairbanks, Alaska. This unique museum is a top tourist attraction for visitors from around the world. After retiring from employment at the U.A. Museum of the North in 2005, she married her long-ago, high school boyfriend, Reford (Jeep) Reid. They continue to enjoy life together in Alaska.

Her first publications were two stories in *Highlights for Children* magazine under her former name Marie Delilah Ward. Following are current novels by her. Each book is perfect for readers of about 12 years and up. All are available from Amazon or Barnes and Noble in paperback or ebook.

Author may be contacted on Facebook, or email at alaskastory4@gmail.com.

YOUNG ADULT NOVELS BY MARIE OSBURN REID

OVER RAINBOWS is a mystery in early Alaska! An orphaned young girl tells about sailing to Alaska in 1925 to fulfill their father's dying wish. Her sister is promised to be the bride of a wealthy gold miner. An evil force follows them on sea, land, and in the air as they work to solve a murder. Their lives revolve around a bush pilot, pioneer, mystic, gambler and friends. Inspired by the thrill of aviation, their adventure brings life threatening danger and sparks of love. This is an exciting novel for anyone who enjoys a fast moving mystery.

CLIMBING THE GREAT DENALI With their mountaineering coach, teenagers Mitch and Jason aspire to climb America's highest mountain, known as the native name Denali. Before 1956, the mountain was labeled with the previous authorized name, Mt. McKinley. The climb for Mitch is to inspire a bed-ridden child to work for recovery after losing a leg to a drunk driver. The inspiration for Jason is to replicate the task of his Native ancestor, the first known to reach the summit. The peak is at 20,320 feet, a climb full of adventure and life threatening events. This novella is great for readers of any age who want to know about mountain climbing in frigid Alaska, especially Mt. Denali.

WHISPERS TO A DEAF DOG A bear attacks, ice on the Yukon River breaks open, a mother moose charges, races begin for energetic sled dogs. A very special dog leads the way and saves lives. Experiences are either told by Brooke Anne or by James. Their adventures as teenagers bring danger, outstanding dogs, tests of culture, and a glimpse of lives evolving. This novella is exciting for anyone who loves a dog and wants to know about racing sled dogs.

41532789R00109

Made in the USA
Lexington, KY
09 June 2019